THE
FIRE
WITHIN

CHRIS D'LACEY

SCHOLASTIC INC.

NEW YORK TORONTO LONDON AUCKLAND SYDNEY
MEXICO CITY NEW DELHI HONG KONG BUENOS AIRES

ISBN 0-439-83019-2

12 11 10 9 8 7 6 5   6 7 8 9 10/0

Printed in the U.S.A.   40

This edition first printing, September 2005

The text type was set in Sabon.

Book design by David Caplan

For Jay,

who had the first Snigger

and will almost certainly have the last laugh

◆　◆　◆

I would like to thank the following for their

help in bringing this book to life Bat

and Puff, dragons of the first

flight, and Val Chivers,

for kilning

Zookie

Clays are extraordinary, layered, crystal structures which have, built into them, what amounts almost to an innate tendency to evolve. . . . Clay has plans.

Lifetide by Lyall Watson
(Hodder & Stoughton, 1979)

ORIGINALLY FROM *AN INTRODUCTION TO CLAY COLLOID CHEMISTRY*
BY H. VAN OLPHEN (INTERSCIENCE PUBLISHERS, NEW YORK, 1963)

4 Thoushall Road
Blackburn, MA

Mrs. Elizabeth Pennykettle
42 Wayward Crescent
Scrubbley, Massachusetts

Dear Mrs. Pennykettle,

Help! I am desperately in need of somewhere to stay. Next week, I am due to start a Geography course at Scrubbley College and I haven't been able to find any housing.

I am scrupulously clean, and as tidy as anyone of my age (20) can be. My hobby is reading, which is generally pretty quiet. I get along very well with children and I love cats.

Yours sincerely,

David Rain

Mr. David Rain

P.S. I'm afraid I haven't seen any dragons around lately.
I hope this isn't a problem.

PART ONE

THE SPARK

WELCOME TO WAYWARD CRESCENT

Well, here we are," Mrs. Pennykettle said, pausing by the door of the room she had for rent. She clasped her hands together and smiled. "Officially, it's our dining room, but we always eat in the kitchen these days."

The young man beside her nodded politely and patiently adjusted his shoulder bag. "Lovely. Erm, shall we take a look . . . ?"

"It used to be our junk room, really," said a voice.

Mrs. Pennykettle clucked like a hen.

The visitor turned. A young girl was lolling in the kitchen doorway. She was dressed in jeans and a sloppy top and had wet grass sticking to the heels of her sneakers. "All our junk's in the attic now."

"And where have *you* been?" Mrs. Pennykettle said.

"In the garden," said the girl, "looking for Conker."

"Conkers?" the young man queried. "Aren't you a week or two early for them?"

"Not *ers*," said the girl, "*er*."

The visitor furrowed his brow.

Mrs. Pennykettle sighed and did the introductions: "David, this is Lucy, my daughter. I'm afraid she comes as part of the package. Lucy, this is David. He's here to see the room."

Lucy chewed a wisp of her straw-colored hair and slowly looked the visitor up and down.

Her mother tried again: "We did the best we could with the room. There's a table in the corner, with a study lamp, of course, and a wardrobe we bought from a secondhand shop. The bed isn't great, but you should be all right if you try to avoid the loose spring in the middle."

"Mom?"

"*What?*"

"Why don't you stop twittering and *show* him?"

2

With a huff, Lucy stomped down the hall to join them. "She's not always like this," she said to David. "It's because we've never had a tenant before." Before her mother could "twitter" in protest, Lucy reached out and pushed the door open. David smiled graciously and stepped inside. The fresh smell of lavender wafted through the room, mingled with the peaceful tinkle of wind chimes. Everything was perfect, exactly as described. Except . . .

"What's that?" David pointed to a bulge in the bed.

Elizabeth Pennykettle groaned with embarrassment. She swept across the room and dived beneath the folds of the red patterned blanket.

"That's Bonnington, our cat," Lucy said, grinning. "He likes getting under things — newspapers, blankets, all sorts of stuff. Mom says he's always getting under her feet."

David smiled and put down his bag. "Bonnington. That's a really good name for a cat."

Lucy nodded in agreement. "Mom named him after a mountain climber. I don't know why; he couldn't climb a beanbag. Well, he *could*, but we don't have one. He mistakes the sound of the beans for cat litter, then he poops on there instead of in his box."

"Lovely," said David, glancing anxiously at the blanket.

With a rake of claws against fresh bed linen, Mrs. Pennykettle emerged clutching a brown tabby cat. Her curls of red hair, now in total disarray, resembled a rather bedraggled mop. She grimaced in apology, plopped Bonnington on the windowsill and bundled him ungracefully into the garden.

David moved the conversation on. "Are there buses to the college from here?"

"Loads," said Lucy.

"Three an hour," her mother confirmed, hastily replumping her hair. "And there's room in the shed for a bike, if you have one. If you were stuck, you could always have a lift into town in my car — as long as you don't mind sharing with the dragons."

"Oh yes," said David, raising a finger. His mind floated back to the wording on the postcard in the newsstand window: MUST LIKE CATS AND CHILDREN AND . . .

"Like him." Lucy pointed to a shelf above a sealed-off fireplace. Sitting at its center was a small, clay dragon, unlike any that David had ever seen. It wasn't a fearsome, fire-breathing monster, the sort of dragon that might capture medieval maidens. Nor was it a cutesy, cartoon sort of thing. There was a fiery pride in its oval-shaped eyes as if it had a sense of its own importance and knew it had a definite place in the world. Its tall slim body was painted green with turquoise hints at the edges of its scales. It was sitting erect on two flat feet and an arrow-shaped tail that swung back on itself in a single loop. Four ridged wings (two large, two small) fanned out from its back and shoulders. A set of spiky, flaglike scales ran the entire length of its spine.

David picked it up — and very nearly dropped it. "It's warm," he said, blinking in surprise.

"That's because —"

"It's been in the sun too long," said Mrs. Pennykettle,

quickly cutting her daughter off. She lifted the dragon out of David's hands and rested it gently back on the shelf. A cone of sunlight fell across it.

"There are loads of dragons in our house," said Lucy, a bubble of excitement in her voice.

David smiled and touched a finger to the dragon's snout. For one strange moment he thought he could detect a layer of ash on the wide, flared nostrils. He ran a thumb across the glaze and decided it was dust. "Do you collect them?"

Lucy shook her ponytail. "We make them."

"*I* make them," said her mother.

"I'm learning," said Lucy. "*Pennykettle Pots and Crafts*. We're famous. Mom sells them at the market on Tuesday and Thursday and Saturday afternoons. When there's a craft fair at Scrubbley Garden Center she takes some there. Lots of people buy them."

"I bet," said David, with a nod of admiration. "Do you make them here?"

Mrs. Pennykettle pointed at the ceiling. "I have a small studio in one of the bedrooms."

6

"It's called the Dragons' Den," Lucy said mysteriously. She put her hands behind her back and swung her shoulders. "*You're* not allowed to enter."

"Lucy, don't tease," her mother chided. Turning to David again she said, "I'll gladly show you around once you've settled in — well, if you decide to take the room, that is."

David ran a hand through his mop of brown hair. Dragons. It was certainly different from his last place, where all you got were spiders and the occasional mouse. "It's perfect," he said. "Just what I want. If you and your dragons will have me, Mrs. Pennykettle, I'd like to move in right away."

"Call me Liz," she said, holding out a hand. "We'd love for you to stay. Wouldn't we, Lucy?"

Lucy wiggled her nose. "That depends — on the other thing."

"Other thing?" said Liz. "What other thing?"

Lucy smiled directly at David and said, "Do you like —?"

SETTLING IN

Peas?" said Mrs. Pennykettle, cutting in again. "We're having shepherd's pie for dinner. Could you eat a few peas?"

"Erm, yes," said the tenant, looking slightly confused.

Lucy squared up to her mother and hissed, "Mom, you know I wasn't going to say *peas!*" She made a grumpy-sounding *hmph!* and turned on her heels. "I'm going out to look for Conker again."

"I don't think so," said her mom, catching hold of her shoulders. "You're going to help me peel potatoes." She pushed Lucy to the door like a shopping cart. "We'll leave you to settle in, David. If there's anything you need, don't hesitate to call. Dinner in about an hour, OK?"

"Great," he said, smiling politely, still wondering what Lucy had been intending to say. Instinct warned him not to ask. Instead, he pursued a more urgent matter: "Excuse me, where's the bathroom?"

"Top of the stairs, turn left," said Liz. "Remind me to find some towels for you later."

David nodded. "I'll be quick." He glanced at Lucy as he stepped into the hall.

"It's not fair," she complained, folding her arms.

"Kitchen," said her mom.

And that was that.

With a shake of his head, David started up the stairs. If first impressions were anything to go by, life with the Pennykettles promised to be an interesting, if slightly unusual, experience. Proud-eyed dragons. A dippy cat. Wind chimes at the window. Someone called Conker — whoever he was. And now this . . .

He slowed to a halt at the top of the stairs, his eye drawn to a sign on a door across the landing:

DRAGONS' DEN

It was hand-painted, gold and green, with bright orange flames leaping up around the lettering. David drummed his fingers on the banister rail. The desire to have a peek inside was enormous. But the door to the studio was firmly closed, and if Liz came up and caught him sneaking, it would be good-bye Mr. Rain — and no shepherd's pie, either. Casting temptation aside, he went into the bathroom and switched on the light.

There he met his second dragon.

It was sitting on the toilet tank. It was bluer in color than the dragon downstairs — to tone with the bathroom, he thought. It had smaller wings, a longer snout and a rather peculiar, *alert* expression. It wasn't warm like the other but it did have a faintly *rosy* smell as if its glaze had been specially painted to carry some sort of freshening scent. David turned it to face the wall. No way was he going to unzip himself — not with that thing watching.

By dinnertime, Liz and Lucy had forgotten their tiff and David was made to feel fully at home. He had two large helpings of shepherd's pie, a slice of cheesecake and a glass of ginger beer. The peas, he declared, were the best he'd ever tasted. Afterward, everyone moved into the living room. Bonnington, his best seat taken by the tenant, even curled up in David's lap.

Lucy Pennykettle talked nonstop. She wanted to know *everything* about the tenant. More importantly, she wanted the tenant to know everything about *her*. David listened patiently. He learned all about Lucy's progress at school, what her friends were going to think of her mom having a *tenant* and what Lucy was going to be when she grew up.

"Less of a chatterbox than you are now, I hope," her mother put in.

"I'm going to be an acrobat," Lucy announced. "I'm going to wear a leotard and swing on a trapeze. Do you want to see my handstand?"

"Of course he doesn't," said her mom.

Lucy shrugged, undeterred, and said to David, "I'm going to save animals as well. Do you *like* animals?"

11

"I like cats," he replied, even though Bonnington was giving him a cramp.

A sparkle entered Lucy's eye. "Do you like squirrels?"

"Lucy, it's past your bedtime," said her mom.

Lucy frowned and glanced at the clock. "Do you?" she pressed, nudging David's toe.

"Lucy," said her mom, "you've talked him half to sleep as it is. He doesn't want to be pestered about squirrels."

Lucy said hotly, "I was only asking if he *liked* them, Mom."

"The red ones are pretty," David put in, trying to defuse the argument a little. By now he'd figured out that squirrels were "the other thing" Lucy had been wanting to ask about earlier.

Surprisingly, Lucy looked at him in shock. "Don't you like the gray ones?"

"Lucy, if you want a story tonight you'd better get up those stairs right now."

"Please say you like the gray ones," Lucy whispered. Her bright green eyes were wide and pleading.

"I like the gray ones," David obliged her. Then, lowering his voice a little he asked, "Is Conker a squirrel?"

"Yes!"

"Bed. Now." Liz dropped her magazine and pushed up her sleeves.

Lucy seemed to take this as a final warning. She grabbed her sweater off the couch and hurried to the door. "Night, night," she chirped, and pounded up the stairs.

As her footsteps faded into the distance, David glanced sheepishly at Liz and said, "Sorry, was I not supposed to mention . . . y'know?"

Liz smiled and shook her head, partly with amusement, part exasperation. "Lucy loves wildlife, particularly squirrels. This morning we agreed that if you took the room she wouldn't pester you about them for at least a day. Her timing was a little off, as usual. I was trying to spare you, as it's your first night."

"I don't mind," said David. "She's quite funny, really."

"Hmm, you say that now," said Liz. "I guarantee by the end of the week you'll be wishing that Noah had never let them on the ark." She stood up and tugged the curtains shut, taking care not to topple a gruff-looking dragon that was standing on top of a small speaker.

David ran a knuckle down Bonnington's back. "It's very leafy around here. You must see lots of squirrels."

To David's surprise, Liz gave a shake of her head. "Not now. Not since the oak tree's been gone."

David lifted an eyebrow. "You had an oak? In the garden?"

"In the Crescent. Next door to Mr. Bacon's. He's our neighbor, on this side." Liz pointed at the chimney wall. "It was cut down a few months ago. We got a note under the door, saying its roots were damaging the road. It didn't look all that bad to me, but someone must have known what they were doing, I suppose. Lucy was devastated. Cried for days. When the tree went, the squirrels went too. She's been looking for them ever since."

"Conker," said David, latching on. "She was looking for him when I arrived."

"Yes, he's the only one she's seen so far. I think they've scattered all over. There's nothing in the Crescent for them now."

David's eyebrows narrowed a little. "So, why is Conker still around? If the rest have scuttled off, why hasn't he?"

Liz stooped to gather Lucy's shoes. "Lucy says he's hurt and can't get away."

"Hurt?" David sat up a little straighter. Bonnington, wakened by the sudden movement, gave a fishy-smelling yawn and dropped to the floor.

Liz opened the door to let the cat out. "He's only got one eye," she said.

MEET
MR. BACON

The following afternoon, the bulk of David's things arrived. It all came in boxes — lots of boxes — delivered by a van marked DONNELLY'S PEST CONTROL SERVICES. Brian Donnelly was the father of one of David's friends, though no one in Wayward Crescent knew that. There were some snooty looks from a few of the neighbors, who all seemed to be wondering why a pest control van had pulled up outside the Pennykettle house.

Elizabeth Pennykettle took no notice. She even stood guard beside the van while David and Mr. Donnelly carried the boxes inside.

And that was how Mr. Bacon found her — on guard, but off guard, so to speak.

"Fleas?" he whispered in her ear.

"Hhh!" cried Liz, with a hand to her chest. She groaned loudly when she saw who it was. Liz and Henry Bacon didn't always get along. "Do you mind?" she said haughtily. "You made me jump."

"One of the signs," Mr. Bacon said. He pursed his lips. His gray mustache twitched. "Tricky little pests, fleas. Jump up to forty times their own height, you know. Give your ankles some nasty bites. Red blotches everywhere. Itch terribly at night, they do."

Liz wriggled uncomfortably and scratched at her arms.

"Creeping, are they?" Henry went on. "They'll be heading for your neck. Up the sleeves and straight for the neck. Knew a man once who had one in his ear. If you want my advice, you'll make that thing wear a collar in the future."

A dark cloud crossed Mrs Pennykettle's face. "What *thing*?"

"That mangy old cat."

"I beg your pardon!"

David wandered out to the van at that moment.

17

"What's the matter?" he asked, spotting the flush on his landlady's face.

"Meet Mr. Bacon, our neighbor," she said, ever so slightly grinding her teeth. David said hello. Mr. Bacon tipped his hat. "Mr. Bacon thinks Bonnington is riddled with fleas." Liz tilted her head towards the van.

David quickly put two and two together. "Don't think so," he hummed. "I haven't seen him scratching. Mind you, he could have picked them up from that rat I just saw in next door's garden."

"RAT?!" cried Mr. Bacon.

"On which side of us do you live, Mr. Bacon?"

Mr. Bacon didn't answer. He was off as fast as his legs could carry him. He went so fast his hat flew off. David picked it up before Liz could flatten it.

"Is it true?" she asked. "Did you really see a rat?"

David put the hat on Mr. Bacon's gatepost. "Have you ever seen a rat with a big fluffy tail?"

Liz shook her head.

"Me neither," said the tenant. "What I saw was a squirrel."

DAVID
UNPACKS

Y ou saw him!" cried Lucy, bursting into David's room the moment she arrived home from school that day.

David tottered slightly and looked over his shoulder. He was balancing on a stool, stacking books on a shelf. All around the room were half-opened boxes, packed with an assortment of dusty bits and pieces: magazines, CDs, posters, a radio, a plastic model of the space shuttle, a travel alarm clock, an expensive-looking camera, a personal computer and a tiny mountain of books.

"Saw who?" he asked.

"Conker!" Lucy wriggled her backpack onto the floor and blew a loose strand of hair off her brow. She hurried to the window, raised herself on tiptoe and

19

peered intently into the garden. "Mom told me," she continued, practically breathless. "You fibbed to Mr. Bacon. You said you saw a rat, but you really saw Conker."

David blew a cloud of dust off a book. "I saw a squirrel; I couldn't swear it was Conker. He was pretty far off — near Mr. Bacon's pond. Conker's the squirrel with one eye, isn't he?"

Lucy leaned back, hands first, against the wall. "Yes," she said. "How did you know?"

"I read minds," said David in a spooky voice. He wiggled his outstretched fingers at her.

Lucy wasn't swayed. "Mom told you," she sniffed. "That's not fair. Conker's *my* squirrel."

"Conker's a wild animal," said David. "He doesn't belong to anyone, Lucy." He stepped down off the stool and picked up another handful of books. "How come you have a name for him, anyway? I would have thought it's practically impossible to tell one squirrel from another."

Lucy hurried across the room, pushed an old guitar

into the middle of the bed and plopped herself down. "It is, unless you look hard. I had names for five of them. Should I tell you?"

"Well —"

"OK. First there was Conker. I called him that because of the red tufts of fur around his feet. All the squirrels had those but his were sort of *browner*, like a chestnut."

"Very good," said David. He picked his space shuttle out of a box and looked around for somewhere to land it.

"Then there was Ringtail. He was easy to see: He had some whirly black fur on his tail. And Cherrylea, she was ever so pretty. I named her after a can of rice pudding."

"Rice *pudding?*"

"I like it; we have it all the time."

"Great," muttered David, who wasn't particularly fond of it. He put his shuttle on the fireplace shelf, and for the first time noticed something was missing. "Oh, the dragon's gone."

Lucy nodded, pulling up a sock. "Mom must have taken him back to the den."

"Why? I liked him."

Lucy turned and glanced at the open window. A warm breeze was rippling the curtains, making the wind chimes tinkle softly. "It's probably because . . . I don't know," she said awkwardly. "How many names have I done?"

"Conker, Ringtail and Cherrylea," muttered David, wondering why Lucy had looked at the window. Seeing nothing out of the ordinary, he shrugged and continued unpacking.

"I forgot Shooter," Lucy prattled on, prying the flaps on a box beside her. "He buried his acorns in Mr. Bacon's lawn and Mr. Bacon didn't like it, 'cause his lawn grew oak trees. What's in here?"

"A ferocious crocodile."

Lucy squealed and pulled away — then risked a peek. "It's books," she pouted.

"Good job," said David, tapping her nose, "or *this*

might have been bitten right off." He put some ring binders on the bed. "What was the fifth squirrel called?"

Lucy almost leapt into the air as she said it: "Birchwood. He used to chase the others away. He had a big white tummy and his fur was sparkly, like the bark of a silver birch tree. I hope he went far away. He was always fighting."

David nodded, taking this in. "Maybe that's how Conker's eye got hurt — Birchwood, fighting?"

Lucy thought for a moment, then shook her head. "He didn't really fight; he just growled and spat and the others ran away. He was a bully. I didn't like him much. Can I look at your teddy bear, please?" She pointed to a bear's snout, just visible behind some rolled-up posters.

David hauled a golden-haired teddy from a box.

"What's his name?"

"Winston. Be careful, his left ear's loose."

Lucy gave the bear a cuddle. "Does he sleep in your bed?"

"Only if he promises not to snore. What about Bonnington? Didn't *he* chase the squirrels?"

Lucy swung her ponytail. "He used to sit on the fence and watch them sometimes, but he never pounced. He wouldn't scratch eyes."

"Hmm," went David, not entirely convinced. "How bad is Conker's injury? Have you seen it? Up close?"

Lucy sat forward with Winston on her knee. "He came to the bird feeder once and I sneaked up behind him to feed him some peanuts — and that's how I saw it. It was closed — like this." She shut one eye as tightly as she could. "I called his name and he jumped and got frightened. But instead of running away, he went around and around in circles on the grass. I kept turning to watch him — but I got dizzy and fell over. When I stood up again, he wasn't there. He went around my legs *three* times — no, four. Are you going to help me rescue him?"

"Rescue him? How do you mean?"

"I want to take him where Ringtail and Cherrylea went."

The tenant spluttered with laughter. "Lucy, you can't go catching wild squirrels."

"But he's sick," she pressed, flapping Winston's paw for added effect. "He's getting thinner. You can see his bones. And what if the thing that hurt him comes back? What if it gets his *other* eye? You said you liked squirrels. Oh, *please* help me save him."

David shook his head and turned back to his boxes. "It's not right to interfere with nature, Lucy. Besides, you don't have any idea where Ringtail and the others have gone."

"Somewhere nice," she muttered, more in hope than expectation. She lowered her head and swung a leg in defeat.

"Look," said David, bopping her knee with a rolled-up poster. "If I thought that Conker was really in danger — I mean *really* in danger — I'd do everything I could to help him, OK? But I think you're fretting too much. Chances are he's coping just fine. Come on, cheer up. Do you want to do me a favor?"

"What?" said Lucy, sounding rather deflated.

"Run and ask your mom if I can borrow a duster."

Lucy shook her head. "She shouldn't be disturbed. She's upstairs, making you a dragon."

"Not anymore, she isn't," said a voice. Liz came bumping through the door, carrying a tray of tea and cookies. She was wearing jeans and an artist's smock. There were smudges of clay all over the material, but mostly the smock was daubed with paint. Bright green paint.

The color of dragons.

UNUSUAL THINGS

I hope you're not pestering him again," said Liz, kneeling and setting the tray on the floor.

"My fault," said David, getting in first. "I was asking if she knew how Conker's eye got hurt."

Liz hummed as if her point was proven anyway. She handed Lucy a glass of milk.

David switched the subject away from squirrels. "I hear you've been making me a dragon?"

"Just a little housewarming gift," said Liz.

"It's a special one," Lucy put in. "I've got two: Gawain and Gwendolen." (She pronounced the second dragon's name Gawendolen.)

David, mystified as always when the talk turned to

dragons, heaped a spoonful of sugar into his tea and said, "What do you mean, 'special'?"

Lucy looked up. "They're —"

"Little reflections of their owners," said Liz. "Help yourself to a cookie, David." She pushed the plate so close to his face he could almost eat a cookie without having to pick one up. He smiled and took a graham cracker. Lucy sank back looking miffed. She grabbed a cookie and chomped it hard.

"When I make someone a special dragon," Liz continued, "I try to bring out some . . . quality or interest of the person concerned. If you were fond of baseball, for instance, I might make one holding a bat."

"He likes books," said Lucy, picking up a large, spiral-bound volume. It had a bleak gray mountain range on the cover. She turned a few pages and put it down, bored.

"That's a textbook — for college," David said. "I do read other things: stories and stuff."

Lucy sat up smartly. "Would you read one to me?"

"Lucy!" snapped her mother. "That's very cheeky."

"I have a story every night," Lucy went on regardless. "Mom tells me about the dragons."

David glanced at the ceiling as if it were a window to the den above. "I'm impressed: a storyteller *and* a potter?"

"They're hardly best-sellers," Liz said modestly. She raised a hand before Lucy could speak. "Go upstairs, please, and change out of those clothes. And while you're up there, check on David's dragon."

Lucy sighed and wriggled off the bed. Her feet had barely touched the floor when there came a dreadful shrieking sound from the garden. Everyone turned to the open window, in time to see Bonnington come scrambling in. The big tabby cat had his ears laid back and his fur sticking out like the branches of a tree. He dropped to the floor, flattened his back and quickly wriggled under the bed.

"What is the matter with him?" said Liz.

David walked to the window and opened it wide. Loud bird chatter filled the room.

"Go and see!" hissed Lucy, tugging David's sleeve. "Conker might be in danger!"

David raised an eyebrow, and went to have a look.

In the garden, all seemed peaceful enough. David walked one side of the long, narrow lawn, stopping here and there to sweep back leaves on the larger plants. He couldn't find anything out of place, other than a broken plant pot. His heart did leap when he poked around in some overgrown grass and heard a momentary squishing noise. But that turned out to be a soggy old sponge. He checked the rock garden, the shed, the trash area and an old pane of glass covered in algae. He even scrabbled up the paneled fence to have a quick look over into Mr. Bacon's garden. There was no sign of squirrels, and nothing to suggest any inkling of danger.

But on the way back to the house, he did make two important discoveries. Near the patio steps he crouched down and picked up a blue-black feather. It was long and sleek and felt cool against his skin. It belonged to a jay — or a crow, perhaps? Was it possible that Bonnington had clashed with a bird? David's gaze panned the autumn skyline, taking in the spreading sycamore tree that stood in the gap between the Pennykettles' house and Mr. Bacon's away to the right. He couldn't see a black-colored bird anywhere, but as his eyes drifted back toward the house he did see something that made him start. A light had just flickered in the Dragons' Den. A few seconds passed, then it flickered again, flooding the window with a pale orange color. David cupped a hand above his eyes. It seemed too precise to be sunlight on glass, too irregular to be a candle glow. And a lightbulb, he decided, was really the wrong color. Which left just one explanation.

"Fire . . ." he breathed, and let the feather go.

It had barely touched the ground by the time he burst, breathless, into his room.

A Very Special Dragon

W hat on earth?" said Liz as the door crashed open. She put her hand on the teapot to steady it.

"Fire!" cried David. "Upstairs! Quickly! Dial 911! I'll get water from the bathroom!"

"Fire?" said Lucy, looking quizzically at her mom.

"I saw it from the garden! Come on, Liz! Hurry!"

"David, wait," she cried, grabbing his arm. "Slow down. I think you're mistaken."

Lucy, by now, was moving to the door. "I'll go and have a look."

"What?!" screeched David. "*She* can't go!"

But Lucy was already climbing the stairs.

"David, calm down," Liz said, restraining him.

"That's my studio. There's nothing that could cause a problem."

Seconds later, Lucy called down from the landing, "It's all right, Mom. It's only . . . y'know."

"What?" said David, looking baffled. "I saw a jet of flame. I'm sure I did."

Liz smoothed the creases she'd made in his sweatshirt. "Probably a dragon sneezing," she said. "Come on. Let's go and see how yours is, shall we?"

To David's astonishment, there really was no hint of a fire in the den.

"It was probably this," said Liz. She pointed to a round, stained-glass ornament, dangling off a piece of string in the window. She tilted it to catch the afternoon sun. Jeweled reflections bounced around the room. "Trick of the light," she said.

Suddenly, from behind them, Lucy piped up: "Mom, Gruffen's in the wrong place — again."

David turned. Lucy was staring at a shelf full of

dragons. A look of disapproval was etched on her face. "Who's Gruffen?" he asked.

Liz took him by the arm and twisted him around. "He's a new dragon that sits by the door — usually. The resident dragons — the ones we don't sell — all have their own places. Sometimes they get moved when a new batch goes out. Gruffen always seems to be flitting around. Leave him, Lucy, and come over here."

Lucy trudged over. "Do you like them?" she asked.

In a slightly awed voice, the tenant confessed that he'd never seen anything quite like it before.

All around the studio, arranged on tiers of wooden shelves, were dozens and dozens of handcrafted dragons. There were big dragons, little dragons, dragons curled up in peaceful slumber, baby dragons breaking out of their eggs, dragons in spectacles, dragons in pajamas, dragons doing ballet; dragons *everywhere*. Only the window wall didn't have a rack. Over there, instead, stood a large old bench. A lamp was angled over it. There were brushes and tools and jelly jars prepared, plus lumps of clay beside a potter's wheel. The sweet smell of paint and methyl acetate hung in the air like a potpourri aroma. Now he came to think of it, David realized he'd been smelling the scent from the very first moment he'd entered the house.

"Amazing," he said, gliding over to the bench. "This is a good one, here." He pointed to an eerie but elegant creature on a stand just behind the potter's wheel. It had a wraparound tail and ears like a cat. Two large and exquisitely beautiful wings were rising from its back like sails on a ship. Its oval-shaped eyes were intriguingly closed; its stout front feet pressed firmly together.

"That's Guinevere," said Lucy in a deferential whisper. "She's sort of the queen. She's Mom's special dragon."

"Is she sleeping?"

Lucy gave a shake of her head.

"Praying?"

"Not really."

"What *is* she doing, then?"

35

Across the room, Liz coughed. "Lucy, why don't you show David *his* dragon?"

Lucy pointed to one on the potter's wheel.

David lifted it into his hands. The dragon — his dragon — had all the usual Pennykettle touches: spiky wings, big flat feet, tiled green scales with turquoise flashes. The characteristic oval-shaped eyes had a gentle, cheery, helpful look — but there was deep sensitivity in them too, as if the creature could weep at the drop of a scale. David rested it in his palm. The dragon sat up on its thick, curved tail. Unlike Guinevere, it wasn't praying or resting or whatever the queen dragon was supposed to be doing. Instead, it had a pencil wrapped in its claws and was biting the end of it, lost in thought.

"Hope you like him," said Liz. "He was . . . interesting to do."

"He's wonderful," said David. "Why does he have a pencil?"

"And a pad?" said Lucy, pointing to a notepad in the dragon's other paw.

"It's what he wanted," said Liz, coming to join them. "I tried him with a book, but he just didn't like it. He definitely wanted a pencil to chew on."

"Perhaps he's a drawing dragon," said Lucy. "Do you like drawing pictures?"

David shook his head. "Can't draw for anything. What do you mean, he 'wanted' a pencil?"

Liz lifted a shoulder. "Special dragons are like characters in a book; I have to go where they want to take me. I have a writer friend who's always saying that."

Lucy let out an excited gasp. "You mean he's a dragon for making up stories?!"

"Lucy, don't start," said Liz. "Now, David, if you accept this dragon you must promise to care for him always."

"You mustn't ever make him cry," said Lucy.

David ran a thumb along the dragon's snout. "Erm, this might sound like a silly question, but how is it possible to make him cry?"

"By not loving him," said Lucy, as if it ought to be obvious.

"Imagine that there's a spark inside him," said Liz.

"If you love him, it will always stay lit," smiled Lucy.

"To light it, you must give him a name," said Liz.

"Something magic," said Lucy. "Think of one — now!"

David had a think. "How about . . . Gadzooks?"

Lucy turned on her heels. "They like it!" she said, looking around the shelves.

"They do?" said David, raising an eyebrow. As far as he could tell there were no dragons doing backflips or flapping wings for joy.

Lucy nodded so fast her head looked as if it were in danger of coming right off. "Didn't you hear them going *h* —"

"Gadzooks is a lovely name," said Liz, giving Lucy a nudge with her shoulder. "It suits him very well. Now, tour over. It's time we went downstairs, I think."

"Good idea," said David, wiping a trickle of sweat off his brow. "Is it me or is it getting warm in here? Your oven's not on, is it?"

"It's not dinnertime yet," said Lucy.

"Not the oven in the kitchen," David laughed. "I meant your *potter's* oven. You know, your kiln? When you make things from clay you put them in a kiln to fire, don't you?"

Before anyone could speak, the telephone rang. Liz moved toward the door. "Better answer that." With a curt look at Lucy, she left the room.

No sooner was her mother out of sight than Lucy turned to David and said, "*Are* you going to make up a story for me?"

"No," he said, trying to clean a blemish off Gadzooks. It looked for all the world like a scorch mark on his tail. It was deep in the glaze though. "I'm hopeless at stories, Lucy. I wouldn't have a clue what to tell one about."

"Conker," she suggested, almost bouncing off the floorboards. "Do a story about Conker. Gadzooks will help you. That's what special dragons are for."

David pried his collar away from his neck. It really was getting warm in the den. "No," he said, "but I'll tell you what I *will* do. I've got to go into town on

Friday. While I'm there I'll go to the library and see if I can find a good book about squirrels."

"A storybook?"

"No, a factual one. I'm curious to know how Conker's eye got hurt. A reference book about squirrel behavior might give us a clue."

"All right," said Lucy. "When you know some more, you can do a story then."

"Lucy!" Liz called, before David could respond.

"Coming!" she cried, and ran off. At the door, she paused and looked back at the tenant. "Did you really not hear them *hrring?*"

David looked left and right at the dragons. Dozens of oval-shaped eyes peered back.

Lucy pointed to her heart. "You have to hear it here, before you hear it here." Her finger moved from her heart to her ear. She grinned and skipped away.

"Yeah, right," David muttered, and brought Gadzooks up close to his face. "Hello, dragon. Pilot light lit? Good. Now, listen up. Let's get this relationship straight from the start: no sneezing in the middle

40

of the night, no setting fire to my books or computer and no frightening my teddy bear, OK? Oh, and no crying. First sign of trouble and you turn into a shapeless lump again. Got it?"

Gadzooks chewed the end of his pencil in silence.

David looked around the room a final time. "Hrrr," he went at the shelves of dragons.

Then, clutching Gadzooks, he headed for his room. Still wondering about that kiln.

A VISIT
TO THE LIBRARY

Scrubbley Library was right in the center of town, tucked away on the end of a cul-de-sac that branched off from Main Street. As the front doors glided open, David was pleasantly surprised to find himself in a well-lit, modern building brimming with CDs, computers and videos — and the odd book, of course.

He made his way to the information desk. A balding librarian was sitting behind it, hidden by a large computer screen.

David sat down and pinged the bell. "Excuse me, have you got any books on sq —?"

To his astonishment, Henry Bacon looked up from the computer.

"Oh, it's you," said Henry, flaring a nostril. "'Sq',

did you say? You want me to find you a book on 'Sq'? One of those Asian practices, is it? Like kung fu and tai chi? Can't say I've ever heard of it. Still, we must have something. Section 796.815. Up the stairs. Sharp left. Next!"

"Wait, you don't understand," said David. "When I said 'sq —,' I hadn't finished my sentence."

Henry frowned and sat back in his chair. "This is a very busy library, son. I hope you're not trying to waste my time?"

"I was a little surprised to see you here, that's all."

Mr. Bacon said, "I work here, you fool. Now get to the point. There's someone waiting."

David looked over his shoulder. A young woman with a toddler was standing behind him. "When I said 'sq —,' what I was trying to ask was, could you possibly find me a book on —"

"Squid?" said Henry Bacon, beginning to understand. "You want a book on squid?"

David shook his head.

"Squash?"

"No."

"Squeakers?"

"No!"

"Squints? Squatters? Squaws? Squeegees? Squalls? Squirmy things? Squeezing machines?"

"SQUIRRELS!" David shouted.

"Sssh!" went someone at a nearby table.

David slapped a hand to his face.

"Squirrels?" Mr. Bacon hissed, a disapproving tone in his gravelly voice.

"Gray ones, please," David said pointedly.

Mr. Bacon's faint mustache twitched.

"It's . . . for Lucy. She's doing a project for school."

Mr. Bacon straightened the cuffs of his shirt. He tapped the word "squirrel" into his computer. While he was waiting for the search to complete, he leaned sideways and whispered, "Seen any more of that rat?"

"What rat?" said David, not connecting at first.

"The one in my garden, you idiot."

David's mouth fell open slightly. "Oh, *that* rat," he said, remembering his fib by the pest control van. "No."

Henry pursed his lips. "Doesn't matter. I'm on the case, anyway. Tell Mrs. P. there's nothing to worry about." The computer beeped, drawing Henry's attention. "We appear to have a book called *The World of Squirrels* by A. N. Utter —"

"Great," said David. "Erm, what do you mean you're 'on the case'?"

"— but it's out," said Henry. "We also have *Squirrels and Their Habitats* by G. S. Forage —"

"Good. That'll do. On the case of what?"

"— but that's out as well. Ah, we have *two* copies of *Squirrels in the U.S.A.* by N. K. Graytail —"

"Point me to the shelf," David said tiredly.

"— unfortunately," Mr. Bacon sighed, "they're both in our other branch, in Wiggley."

David groaned and banged his head on the desk.

Mr. Bacon grimaced. He removed a hankie from his jacket pocket and flicked it over the laminated surface.

Just then, the woman with the toddler tapped David's shoulder. "Can I make a suggestion? If you want to learn about squirrels, why don't you just look outside?"

David glanced through the plate glass windows, at the traffic rolling down Main Street.

"The *other* way," Mr. Bacon sighed.

David turned. Through the far library windows he saw treetops swaying in the blustery wind.

The woman said, "Haven't you ever been to the library gardens? Goodness, you must be the only person in Scrubbley who hasn't. Go through the gates at the end of the cul-de-sac. You'll find all the squirrels you want in there."

"Thank you," said David. "I'll go and have a look." He stood up. The woman took his seat. "Mr. Bacon," he said, looking back, "what do you mean, 'Mrs. P.'s got nothing to worry about'?"

But Henry was immersed in his computer once more.

David drummed his fingers and turned away. He had the feeling Mr. Bacon was plotting something, though what, precisely, he couldn't say. All he knew as he exited the library was that something cold had touched him inside. Oddly, he thought about his dragon, then; Gadzooks, sitting on the windowsill at home: a spiky silhouette against the rain-spattered glass. And, in that moment, something peculiar happened. In his mind's eye David saw Gadzooks take his pencil from his mouth and try to scribble something down on his pad. The wind whistled and tugged at David's hair. Ahead of him the treetops bristled and sighed. He shook himself once and Gadzooks disappeared. But as David clanked his way through the tall iron gates and entered the gardens for the very first time, he couldn't shake off the bizarre idea that the dragon had been trying to tell him something.

GREENFINGERS GEORGE

A few paces along the leaf-strewn path that led the way into the gardens proper, David halted by a notice-board which read:

WELCOME TO SCRUBBLEY LIBRARY GARDENS
We hope you enjoy your visit

"Thank you very much," David muttered.

"You what?" a rasping voice replied.

A curious little man stepped out of a clump of laurel bushes.

"Oh — sorry," David called out, turning red. "I didn't realize anyone was here."

The little man wiped his nose on his sleeve. Partly

hidden as he was in the shadow of the trees, he didn't look much bigger than a garden gnome. He was wearing a tattered black padded jacket, and a gray canvas hat with a brim that flopped down like a fraying lampshade. One knee was poking out through his earth-stained pants. On his feet were a pair of work boots that were so big an elephant might have slopped around in them.

David made a stab at proper conversation. "You're not the library gardener by any chance, are you?"

"And what if I was?"

"You might be able to help me. I'm doing a sort of . . . nature study."

The little figure snorted and shuffled around. He went back into the bushes and emerged a moment later with a two-wheeled cart. He bumped it onto the paved path. "People call me 'Greenfingers George' —"

"Pleased to meet you," said David, holding out his hand.

"— but to you, it's Mr. Digwell." George ignored the

handshake, preferring instead to scratch his backside through a hole in his pants. "Well? What is it you want?"

Before David could say, the clock in the library tower bonged three times. David frowned and looked at his watch. It was eleven exactly. "Clock's wrong," he muttered.

"No, it ain't," said George. "Everyone in Scrubbley knows exactly what time it is at three bongs o' the library clock: eleven — one hour before my lunch. I've got half a dozen shrubs to plant by then, so if you want my help you'd better make it quick."

"Squirrels," said David. "Where can I see some?"

"Squirrels?" George trumpeted. "What do you want with them? Pesky little varmints. Bane o' my life. Bite the buds off my saplings, dig up my bulbs, plant their stinking nuts in my lawns. There's one," he said, beckoning David closer, "that lives up the beech near the fountain back there." He pointed vaguely into the distance. "Mean little villain, that one. Plays tricks on me for fun, I reckon. You can't miss him. He's got a *look*."

"A look?" repeated David.

"A great big *smile*."

David cast a doubtful glance toward the fountain.

"Oh, yeah," said George, sucking mud off his finger. "Little pest was in my pottin' shed last week. Stole my ham sandwich, he did."

David did his best to form a sympathetic look. "And where did you say I'd find him — them?"

"Go down the embankment," Mr. Digwell said, pointing along the narrow path that tumbled helter-skelter through the thicket of trees, "all the way to the fencin' at the bottom. Take the left-hand path around the front of the bandstand and keep going over the duck pond bridge. Go through the clearing where the big oak stands, and the beeches are right on up from there."

David gave a cordial nod and crunched off down the path. He'd gone less than five paces when he turned and said: "Mr. Digwell, can I ask you something else?"

The gardener sighed and leaned on a pitchfork.

"How might a squirrel lose an eye?"

George muttered something under his breath. He lifted his fork and forced it ominously into the ground. "Could be any number o' reasons. Accident. Disease. Likeliest cause is somethin' attacked it."

"A cat?"

"Yeah, maybe. Tomcat'd most likely kill it, though. They don't take many prisoners, cats."

David nodded. Maybe Bonnington wasn't as dippy as he looked. "What about another squirrel?"

George beat his chest and spat a glob of phlegm into a leaf-blocked drain. "Nah. Squirrels, they squabble and bluster a lot, pull out fur, bite toes, perhaps. But an eye? No, that's somethin' bigger. Fox. Dog. Man, maybe."

David looked at the gardener, hard.

George threw his pitchfork into the bottom of the cart. "Tree rats ain't a protected species. If they're a nuisance, boy, people remove 'em." He drew a sharp line across his neck.

"What sort of people?" David asked.

"People who don't like pests," said George. "Now, if you have no more questions, I've got my plantin' to do." And pushing his two-wheeled cart ahead of him, he strode off down the winding path, until he was no bigger than another dead leaf, tumbling out of the autumn sky.

THE WISHING FOUNTAIN

When the gardener was out of sight, David set off in search of the beech trees. He followed the path around as George had suggested until the ground leveled out at the foot of the embankment and the path split into two. To his left, the bandstand poked into view, half hidden by a weeping willow. To his right was another large bank of trees. In front of him now was a sun-speckled pond. Mallards and rails were resting near the shore. A few paddleboats were moored to a makeshift dock. David clattered across the narrow arched bridge and strolled into the clearing toward the great oak. The ground there was littered with acorns, many still wedged into their knobby gray cups. David crouched down and picked one up. It was greenish brown and not quite firm — softened, perhaps, by early morning dew. He jiggled it in the palm of his hand. He began to think then about Wayward Crescent and the oak tree that had once stood there. What was Conker eating if it wasn't acorns? Peanuts from a bird feeder? Bacon rinds? Did he have a secret cache of nuts? Was it because of a fight for food that his eye had become so badly hurt? David sighed and dropped the acorn back into the ferns. How could he really hope to find out?

He was still pondering the question some ten minutes later when he stumbled upon a small, stone fountain halfway up a rise called Cobnut Hill. He peered into the glistening, leaf-covered water. Coins of varying size and value were lying against the blue-tiled bottom. David found a penny and flipped it in the air. As it spun, he found himself wishing he knew what he could do to best help Conker. With a *sploop,* the penny hit the surface of the water. It sank with a gentle skating motion. As it settled on the bottom, David heard a faint noise. He looked to the opposite side of the fountain. A keen-eyed squirrel was sitting on the wall.

Without a moment's hesitation, it scuttled around the stonework and stopped within a meter of David's hand.

"Hello," said David.

The squirrel flagged a lively, white-tipped tail. It lifted one foot and twitched its nose. It looked at David as if to say "feed me." David put a hand in his coat pocket and produced the only item of food he possessed: a small red apple.

The squirrel scratched its ear with a thumping back foot.

Then it sat back on its haunches — and *smiled*.

David nearly fell into the fountain in astonishment. Perhaps it was the shape of the squirrel's mouth, giving the impression of a cheesy grin, but it really did look as if the creature had smiled.

"It's you," said David. "The sandwich robber. I was warned about you."

The squirrel, unconcerned by its notoriety, bristled its whiskers and edged a little nearer. It looked hard at the apple and its nose twitched again. It put a long, clawed foot on David's thigh.

David crunched softly into the fruit, chewed off a piece and dropped it on the wall.

The squirrel leaned forward and took it . . . then promptly spat it into the fountain.

David frowned like a disappointed parent. "Don't tell me — you prefer *Granny Smiths?*"

The squirrel chose not to smile at that. It fidgeted, impatiently, left and right, then sat up cautiously and sniffed the air.

Suddenly, with a chatter of alarm, it was gone.

"Hey, what's the matter?" David called.

The cause of the problem soon became apparent.

Another squirrel was on the wall. It was big enough to be a baseball on legs. Its tail alone was like a small feather boa. With a passing sneer at the visiting human, it scrabbled off the fountain and chased the first squirrel across the path.

"Hey!" cried David. "Leave him alone."

But the smiling squirrel didn't need any help. It was up a tree and gone before David had time to take another breath. He shrugged and decided to leave them to it. After all, this was probably the sort of tiff that squirrels got into a dozen times a day.

Sploop. Just like the penny dropping into the fountain, a sudden realization hit him. What he just witnessed was a basic example of squirrel behavior: when faced with a nasty encounter, flick tail and run away fast. But the speed of the smiling squirrel's escape, particularly up the tree, was largely due to its remarkable agility, and it couldn't achieve that without peripheral vision. How would it have managed with one eye closed? Could it have climbed as quickly then? Could it have climbed at all? In short, how would Conker have coped if faced with the threat of a bullying squirrel, or marauding cat, or something not yet even imagined?

Somewhere in the distance a mallard quacked.

The answer was as sharp and as clear as that call.

Conker wouldn't cope. He couldn't run from danger.

He was, in effect, a sitting duck.

INSPIRATION

It was late afternoon before David returned to Wayward Crescent. The street lamps were flickering into life and a few dead leaves were skating the pavement. Whistling softly, he opened the gate to Liz's drive. It swung back, not with its usual creak, but with an ear-splitting whine that almost had the tenant jumping into the hedge. He glanced suspiciously at the gate. Either those hinges were in dire need of oiling or . . .

Neee-yaaaaah!

The same whine split the air again. It was someone cutting wood with a high-powered saw.

Someone like Henry Bacon, perhaps.

A light was on in the neighbor's garage. Fueled by

curiosity (but more by suspicion), David crouched low and crept up to the doors. As he raised his face to the grimy window, the thump of a hammer rattled the glass. Something hit the garage floor with a crash. There was a snapping sound. Mr. Bacon cussed. He tossed his hammer onto a workbench. It hit a box of nails and spilled them onto the floor.

David dipped away, frowning hard. Henry was obviously making something. But what, exactly, it was impossible to say. David shook his head and let it pass. There was no law against people doing woodwork in their garages, even if they were as crazy as Henry.

With a shrug, he crossed over onto Liz's drive and let himself into number forty-two. He had barely finished kicking the mud off his shoes when Lucy came sprinting down the hall to greet him.

"Where've you been? School was out ages ago."

"I had lunch with the President and walked his dog around the White House."

"Liar," said Lucy. "Did you get a book?"

A book. David had forgotten the book.

Lucy read the defeated expression on his face. "You did *go* to the library, didn't you?"

"Yes," he said. "Thanks for telling me Mr. Bacon works there." He draped his coat over her head and walked on into the kitchen. "Hmm, something smells good."

Down the hall Lucy shouted: "This coat stinks!"

"Baked potatoes, sausages and baked beans," said Liz, pointing a wooden spoon like a wand. "Simple, but filling. How was your day?"

"Not bad. Spent most of it in the library gard — ow!"

David started with pain as Lucy jabbed him in the thigh with a lollipop stick.

"Hey, that's enough of that," Liz scolded.

"He's being horrible," Lucy complained. "He says I didn't tell him about Mr. Bacon."

"Oh dear. You found Henry?"

"Couldn't miss him," David muttered, glaring at Lucy. "He was at the information desk when I went in specially to get *someone* a squirrel book."

"Where is it?" Lucy badgered, ever hopeful.

"They didn't have one." David flicked a breadcrumb at her.

Lucy made a moody face and thumped into a seat at the kitchen table. On the table was a half-made dragon, a jelly jar of water and a number of sticks. Lucy took a finely pointed stick and began to scrape doggedly at a flat piece of clay. David watched in quiet admiration as she turned it into a three-toed foot.

"So, what did you think of the gardens?" asked Liz.

"Nice," said David, yawning lightly. "I met the library gardener."

"Oh, George. He's been there since the place was opened. They grew him from seed, I think. His wife bought a dragon from me once. He's a funny old guy. A little grouchy, but his heart's in the right place."

"Can't say the same for his timing," David muttered. "He told me this peculiar story about everyone in Scrubbley knowing it's eleven when the library clock strikes three."

"It's true," muttered Lucy. "All the chimes are

wrong. We learn it by heart at school. You have to re-member it never bongs nine."

"That spells doom and gloom," explained Liz.

"Hasn't anyone thought to repair it?"

"Frequently," said Liz, turning sausages with a fork, "but a petition always goes around to leave it be. It's become sort of a tourist attraction. Tricky when the clocks go forward, though."

"You gain four bongs," said Lucy, bending to re-trieve a piece of clay. It was then that David noticed two complete dragons, sitting on the windowsill at Lucy's side. One of them, a rather regal-looking crea-ture, bore an uncanny resemblance to Lucy herself. David looked again from a different angle. The dragon had the usual spikes and scales — and yet, when he stared at it, he clearly saw Lucy. It was almost as if she'd dissolved inside it.

The second dragon, by contrast, was a real monster. Its wings were raised, its jaws were open and its claws were spread in readiness for battle. David peered into its dark green eyes. They had a strangely disconcerting depth. The sort of eyes that could follow you anywhere. He was pleased Gadzooks didn't look like that.

"Who are they?" he asked.

"Gawain and Gwendolen," Lucy muttered.

"What do you think?" asked Liz. She leaned back against the counter, drying pots.

David pointed at the scary one. "Wouldn't like to meet him down a long, dark alley."

"That's Gawain," said Lucy. "He's very *fierce* and he doesn't like *jokes*."

"Don't be grumpy," said Liz. "What about the other one, David?"

The tenant sat down in his usual place and turned Gwendolen around to face him. "At the risk of getting burnt to a crisp, she really reminds me of Lucy —"

Lucy dropped her modeling stick.

"— give or take the odd green scale, of course."

For a moment there was silence. David gave an innocuous smile, hoping he hadn't said anything out of place. You never really knew in the Pennykettle household; dragons were always a ticklish subject. He looked at Lucy. She was gaping at her mom.

Liz dried a plate with a slow, circular motion of the dish towel. "That's very observant," she said. "Not many people can see the resemblance."

"Lucky guess," said David with a nervous shrug. Why did he suddenly get the feeling he'd found the key to some deep, dark secret? He glanced at Gawain and couldn't help but ask, "So if Gwendolen is Lucy, then who's . . . ?"

Lucy's eyes opened to the size of saucers. "He's —"

"Going upstairs," said Liz, just as the timer on the microwave pinged.

"But —?"

"No buts, it's dinnertime. Clear that table."

Lucy's shoulders sagged. She looked once at her half-built dragon, blew it a kiss then squashed it mercilessly into a ball.

Liz pulled on a pair of oven gloves and took three potatoes out of the microwave. She put them on a baking tray and popped them into the oven to crisp. "Five minutes," she said, and whisked outside with a bag of trash.

As the door drifted shut, David tapped Lucy gently on the arm. "Who is he, then?" he whispered, nodding at Gawain.

Lucy bit her lip and glanced outside. "The last dragon in the world," she hissed.

"No. I meant, who's he modeled on?"

Lucy looked at him as if he were an idiot. "He's the last real dragon in the *world*," she repeated.

David, none the wiser, changed the subject. "Fine. Let's talk about Conker. I want to ask you something important. Have you ever seen him climb — since he hurt his eye?"

Lucy looked faintly puzzled.

"Up a tree? Fence? Anything? Think hard."

Lucy thought for a moment, then shook her head. "Why do you want to know?"

"Know what?" said Liz, coming in again. She snatched up a box of cat chow and rattled some into

Bonnington's dish. Bonnington materialized in the kitchen as if he'd beamed down from outer space.

"I was asking Lucy about Conker," said David.

"*Quelle surprise,*" said Liz, making Lucy frown.

David knocked on the table to get her attention. "I saw two squirrels in the library gardens."

Lucy's eyes lit up.

"Lucy, I can still see a mess," said her mom.

Lucy hurried to the sink with her jelly jar and sticks. "What did they look like?" she asked.

"Gray and squirrelly," David said unhelpfully. "One of them was big and fat."

The jelly jar clattered around the sink. "Was it Birchwood?!"

"Birchwood?" David spluttered with laughter. "Not unless he caught the bus to Scrubbley. It's quite a trek to the library gardens."

"Not if you go across the fields," said Lucy. She banged her hands down on the counter. "That's where they went, Mom, the library gardens!"

"Very nice," said Liz. "Now move that clay."

Lucy transferred it to a corner of the counter. "What did the other squirrel look like?"

David put his fingers to the corners of his mouth and pushed his lips up into a grin. "It shmiled, like thish."

Lucy gaped in astonishment. "What's its name?"

"I don't suppose he thought to ask," said Liz. "Cutlery, please."

"Smiler!" Lucy shouted, opening the drawer. "I bet its name is Smiler!" She slapped a fork on the table in triumph.

"That doesn't sound right," said David.

"Well, that was Gawain's turn," Lucy said hotly. "Big Beam, then?"

"Oh dear," clucked Liz. "Imagine being stuck with a name like 'Big Beam'!"

"Well, that was . . . Gwendolen's turn!"

Liz looked at Lucy hard. "Then Gawain and Gwendolen have both gotten it wrong."

Lucy, undeterred, had one last option. "Can Gadzooks have a try?"

"Pardon?" said David.

"Ask him," said Lucy.

"How?" said the tenant, looking bemused.

Lucy paddled her feet. "Dream it," she breathed.

"*What?*" said David.

"Mom, make him do it."

"I'm cooking sausages, Lucy."

"Oh, Mom. Please."

"Do what?" said David.

Lucy threw herself into the chair beside him. "It's Mom's special way of telling stories. You have to join in and tell what you see. Then the story really comes alive. Things happen. Things you don't expect. Oh, Mom, make him *do it.*"

Liz sighed and gave in: "David, close your eyes and picture Gadzooks."

He looked at her askance. "You're not serious?"

"In thirty seconds, your dinner will be burned."

"That's serious," said David. He closed his eyes. "OK. He's on his windowsill, looking out over the garden. I think he's wondering if it's going to rain."

"No," said Liz, "he's biting his pencil, deep in

thought, trying hard to think of a name for your squirrel. Dream it, David."

David rocked in his chair and let his mind float. "He flipped a page of his notepad over."

"Hhh!" gasped Lucy. "It's working, Mom!"

"Shush," went Liz.

"He's writing something."

"What?" gasped Lucy, too excited to be shushed.

David let his imagination flow. To his amazement, he watched Gadzooks take his pencil from his jaws and hurriedly scribble down a name on his pad.

Snigger

David's eyebrows twitched in surprise. Liz prodded a sausage or two with a fork. Lucy bit a fingernail. Bonnington yawned. The whole Pennykettle household waited for an answer.

"Snigger," David whispered.

From somewhere came a gentle *hrring* noise.

David's dark blue eyes blinked open. "Yes," he said, "his name is Snigger."

SOMETHING TRAPPY

I like it," said Lucy, smiling at her mom.

The doorbell rang before Liz could begin to offer an opinion. "Terrific timing," she muttered, turning things down to a lower heat. "Lucy, set the table while I see who that is."

Lucy grabbed the placemats and plopped them down. "Tell me some more about Snigger and Birchwood."

David shrugged. "They went up a tree. That was it."

"*Nooo*," said Lucy. "Make up a story."

"Lucy, I told you, I don't tell stor — hang on." David cocked an ear toward the hall. He could have sworn he had just heard Henry's voice. Now that he'd tuned in, he could certainly hear Liz.

"No," she sighed loudly. "Thank you. Good night."

The door banged shut. She bustled back into the kitchen. "Well, I've heard everything now." She whipped the oven door open. "That was Henry, wanting some gorgonzola."

"That horrible smelly cheese?" said Lucy.

"Why did he want gorgonzola?" asked David, suddenly aware that the hairs on the back of his neck were rising.

"He didn't say," Liz muttered, sliding the potatoes out of the oven. "But, knowing Henry, it's bound to be something typically trappy."

"Oh, no," David gasped, standing up suddenly. His chair legs squealed against the kitchen tiles. "That's it. He's building a . . . Oh, no!" Without another word he was away down the hall.

"Da-vid? What about your dinner?" Liz threw up her hands in despair.

"I'll get him," offered Lucy and went scooting down the hall before her mom could stop her. Ten seconds later, she joined David at the doors of Mr. Bacon's garage.

"Lucy, what are *you* doing here?"

"Why did you run away so fast?"

David gritted his teeth. "Does Mr. Bacon like squirrels?"

"No. He hates them — especially Shooter."

David turned away with a hand across his face. He pushed his hair back hard at the roots. "Go home."

"Why?"

"Because —"

"WHO'S THERE?!"

With a bang, the garage doors opened and Henry leapt out, wielding a golf club.

Lucy squealed and hid behind David's back.

"Stop, Mr. Bacon!" David cried.

"Oh, it's you," said Henry, looking disappointed. He let the club flop tamely to his side. "What are you lurking for, boy? Thought it might be robbers."

David glanced through the open garage door. On the workbench he could see a long narrow box. "What's that?" he said, pointing at it.

A smile touched the corners of Henry's mouth.

74

"Bacon's patented rodent remover. Come and have a look, boy. Work of genius."

"What's a rodent?" asked Lucy, tugging David's sleeve.

"Another name for a rat," he said. "Stay here, Luce. No arguments, OK?"

Lucy looked a little disappointed, but planted herself by the doors anyway.

David followed Mr. Bacon inside.

Henry tapped the box with the heel of his club. "Knocked it out in a couple of hours. Had a little trouble with the spring at first. Works great now. Want to see it in action?"

David crouched down and peered at the contraption. It was made from solid sheets of plywood and was big enough to catch a dozen rats. At the front of the box was a sturdy, hinged door, with a window made from wire mesh. Mr. Bacon pulled it open. It swung upward with a gentle chafing sound. Mr. Bacon hooked it in place with a slim strip of metal screwed to the inner wall of the box. David peered inside. In the far top corner was a covered light, with a small red motion sensor underneath. The only other object was a fine metal wire, dangling from the center of the ceiling of the box. David raised a finger to touch it, and got a golf club across his knuckles for his trouble.

"Safety first," Mr. Bacon hissed. "Finely tuned system. Hair-trigger response. Wire sets it off, boy. That's for the bait. Going to dangle a smelly chunk of cheese on that. Pity Mrs. P. didn't have any. See that?" He pointed the club at the covered light. "Stays on all night to attract the rodent. When Ratty sneaks in, the light blips off. Ratty gropes around in the dark for the bait and . . ." Mr. Bacon prodded the wire with his club. The door came down with a spiteful snap.

Lucy gasped loudly and flapped her fists.

David stood up straight. "Mr. Bacon, stop this. Now."

Henry knitted his wispy eyebrows. "What are you talking about, boy? We can't have Ratty and his chums in the garden."

"But it was Conker!" Lucy shouted, storming in. "David didn't see a rat, he saw a —"

"Cat," said David, clamping a hand across Lucy's mouth. "Conker the cat. Lives four doors up. Slim, gray animal. Easily mistaken for a large rat."

"Cat?" Mr Bacon scoffed. "The only cat around here is the girl's awful beast."

Lucy stamped on David's foot and worked herself free. "I'm going to tell Mom!" She dashed from the garage.

"Lucy, wait!" David called, skipping sideways after her. "Don't do it, Mr. Bacon," he said from the door.

"It's my garden," barked Henry. "I'll do what I like." He swished his golf club to show he meant business.

David hurtled after Lucy. He caught up with her in the hall.

"Get off," she shouted, as he grabbed her shoulder.

"Lucy, listen!"

"Why did you stop me from telling him it was Conker?!"

"Because he doesn't like squirrels! It would only have made things worse!"

"Wrong," said a voice, "it's already worse." The kitchen door opened and Liz was part of the argument as well. "Would someone like to tell me *what* is going on? I don't cook these meals for fun, you know. Your dinner is on the table. If it sits there much longer there'll be frost on it!"

"Mr. Bacon made a rat trap," Lucy wailed. "But there *isn't* a rat! He's going to catch Conker! He's going to kill him! And David *doesn't care!*" She slapped the tenant in the chest, then pounded up the stairs, crying loudly.

Liz folded her arms and glared at him, hard.

"I can explain."

"Don't bother, David. Put a baked potato in it instead." She swept upstairs after Lucy.

It was half an hour before Liz came down. By then, the kitchen was empty. The table was cleared, the dish

78

washing done, and two untouched meals put back in the oven on a very low heat.

Taped to the breadbox, Liz found a message.

Gone for a walk. Took bottles to the recycling bin. Bonnington threw up a hairball. I cleaned it up. Hope Lucy's OK. It's my fault. Sorry. Won't happen again.

David

It was eight before he returned. Liz was in the kitchen, making a drink. "Long walk," she said.

The tenant hovered sheepishly in the hall.

"David, hang your coat up, for goodness' sake. If I wanted you out, you'd have found your teddy in pieces on the step."

David sighed with relief and slipped off his coat. There was a slight clacking sound as he put it on the hook.

"What was that?"

"Oh — my knee against the telephone stool. How's Lucy?"

The kettle clicked off. Liz filled a mug. "Fretting, as you might expect. Actually, you arrived home just in time."

The tenant furrowed his brow.

Liz handed him the mug. "Hot chocolate, for her. Go and make a happy house again. Hmm?"

"Who is it?" said a slightly surprised little voice.

David took his knuckles away from the door. "It's me. Can I come in?"

A blanket rustled. "All right."

David stepped in. Lucy was sitting up in bed, wearing a pair of blue pajamas. Her eyes were red, her cheeks a little blotchy. David put the hot chocolate on her bedside table and sat down on the end of the bed.

"Did you come to read me a story?" she sniffed.

David shook his head. "Not tonight, Luce."

A few seconds passed. Lucy dabbed her nose with a tearstained tissue. "Conker's in danger, isn't he?"

David glanced across the room. The eyes of Gawain stared rigidly back. In the pale yellow glow of the bedside lamp the dragon might well have had fire in its jaws.

"I want to save him," Lucy sniffed. "I don't want Mr. Bacon to catch him in his trap." Her bottom lip shuddered and she started to sob.

David found another tissue and handed it over. "We are going to save him. I've got a plan."

Lucy looked up, her eyes like pools.

"Promise me you won't say a word to your mom?"

Lucy swallowed hard and looked at Gawain. "What are we going to do?"

David glanced away into the corner of the room. "I haven't worked out all the details yet. A lot depends on whether I can find a good box or not."

Lucy's mouth fell open slowly.

"Yes," said the tenant, guessing her thoughts. "If Henry can set a trap, so can we. We're going to try to catch Conker ourselves. . . ."

IN THE ATTIC

The next day, David got his box.

"A rabbit hutch? Where?"

"Up there," hissed Lucy, pointing to a hatch in the landing ceiling. "You open that door and a ladder comes down. Mom shoves all our useless stuff up there."

David ran a nervous hand through his hair. "Your mom'll turn me into useless stuff if she ever finds out I've been rummaging through your attic."

"We'll get it down later when Mom's not here. She's going to a craft fair soon."

Liz's voice rang out from the foot of the stairs: "Lucy, come on, get yourself ready. I want to be out by one."

"I'm not going, Mom. David said he'd help me look for Conker."

"*Lucy?*" David pulled her toward him. "We're supposed to be keeping this quiet, remember?" He clenched his fists and looked over the banister. "Erm, she was so upset last night that I said I'd . . . well . . . y'know."

Liz gave him a green-eyed Pennykettle stare. "I don't know which of you is worse: her for twisting you around her little finger or you for being weaker than the average jellyfish. All right, she can stay. But you're responsible for her. If I come back and find her shoes and jeans caked in mud, you're the one who has to wash them, agreed?"

"Agreed," David groaned, and turned his eyes to the attic.

With the sun streaming in through a dusty skylight, it didn't take long to spot the hutch. It was over in a corner by a couple of cases, with some wallpaper samples and an old roll of carpet. David made his way across the joists, teetering slightly at every step. Lucy, who'd been banned from entering the attic on the grounds that she'd get her jeans dirty, watched from the top of the landing ladder.

"Is it OK?" she asked, as David crouched down to examine the hutch.

"Perfect," he said, dragging it toward him. "Soon we'll — Ooh, what's that?"

"What?" said Lucy, coughing into her fist.

"Light," said David. "Coming in from somewhere. Hang on a sec." He crossed two joists and moved the roll of carpet. A beam of light skimmed the floor of the attic. "There's a hole in the brickwork," David reported, leaning forward for a closer look. "And . . . oh, gosh." His words faded into silence. Lodged in the rafters, close to the hole, was what looked at first like an old bird's nest. But it was bigger than a nest, and rounder too. No bird had made that. It was a squirrel's drey.

"Can I see?" begged Lucy, when David told her.

"No," he said firmly. "You stay there. It looks

abandoned anyway." He crouched lower and squinted out of the hole. "Hah, I can see the sycamore tree. That must be how the squirrel got in; it climbed up the tree then hopped into the roof. Clever. I bet it's really cozy in — *waargh!*"

"Hhh!" squealed Lucy, gripping the ladder as David unexpectedly tumbled backward. A cloud of dust puffed into the air as he landed with a thump that made the ceiling shake.

"Are you all right?" Lucy cried.

"Yes," said David, getting to his feet. He dusted down his clothing and picked up the hutch. "I saw a bird outside. A crow, I think. It landed on a branch while I was looking through the hole. Its eye sort of filled the space. It was dark and beady; made me jump, that's all." He licked a finger and tried to rub a mark off his sweatshirt. "It probably nests around here. I found a crow's feather in the garden once, and — oh, what was that?" He broke off and stared at the attic floor.

"What's the matter?" asked Lucy.

"I heard a fluttering sound downstairs. I think there's something in the Dragons' Den."

"I'll see," said Lucy, hurrying down the ladder.

"Lucy, wait." David clambered down after her. "It sounded like a small bird — a sparrow or something. It's probably best to let me have a look. Here, take this." He handed her the hutch. Then he was past her and into the den.

He peered around the shelves of green-eyed dragons, at Guinevere resting on her stand, at the stained-glass ornament dangling in the window. Nothing remotely birdlike moved. "That's odd," he said. "I'm sure I heard something." He moved closer to the shelves. Lucy dashed in front of him.

"I know!" she exclaimed. "It *was* a sparrow. They shake around in the gutter sometimes. Mom says they have a bath in the dust."

David walked to the window and craned his neck upward. "Hmm. Might have heard an echo in the roof space, I s'pose."

"Yes," said Lucy, looking pleased with herself. "Let's go and do the trap now, shall we?"

David clicked his tongue. "Of course, there is . . . *another* explanation."

Lucy braced herself.

"Could have been a dragon flying around."

Lucy went white and bit her lip.

"I'm joking," David laughed, tousling her hair. "Come on, we've got work to do. Bring a small chunk of clay down, will you?" And he swept through the door, still chuckling to himself.

Lucy breathed a sigh of relief. She let her gaze pan slowly sideways — to the shelf by the door where Gruffen normally sat.

"Typical," she muttered.

The dragon wasn't there.

TO CATCH
A SQUIRREL

As she hurried downstairs to catch up with David, Lucy asked, "Do you think it was Conker who lived in our roof?"

David put the hutch on the kitchen table and swung it around so the cage front was facing him. "If he did, he doesn't now. I'm worried that Conker can't climb very well. If he runs in circles when he's on the ground, imagine what it's like for him trying to climb a tree."

Lucy closed one eye and squinted at the ceiling. "But where does he go when he wants to sleep? Squirrels live up trees."

David unclipped the cage front and pulled it away. Apart from a few old strands of straw, the box was clean and dry inside. "I'd guess he's got a hiding place, low to the ground. And the sooner we find it, the better." He popped the cage front back, then raised the sliding plywood panel that formed the only door of the hutch. He let the panel go. It rattled shut. "Excellent. Did you bring that piece of clay I asked for?"

Lucy plopped a chunk on the table.

David rolled a small piece into a ball. From his pocket he produced a length of string and pressed one end firmly into the ball. He slid the door panel up and used the clay to wedge it open, then he handed Lucy the free end of string. "Pull."

She gave it a tug. The clay came away and the door slid shut.

"Hey, presto," said David, looking pleased. "Not quite as high-tech as Mr. Bacon's, but it just might do the trick."

Lucy still looked a little confused. "But who'll pull the string when the box is in the garden? I have to be in bed by eight o'clock."

"Conker will," said David. "All we have to do is tie your end of the string to a treat and when he picks it up and gives it a tug . . . click. With any luck, we'll have him."

Just then, Bonnington popped in through his cat door. He leapt onto a chair, twitched an inquisitive nose at the hutch and rubbed his cheek along the mesh.

"Hmm," went David, frowning a little. "That's something I hadn't considered: how to keep nosy-paws out?" He mentally measured the entrance to the hutch. The opening wasn't overly big, but any self-respecting cat could easily wriggle in.

"I know!" Lucy said suddenly. She dived into the undersink cabinet and returned with a plastic squeeze bottle. "We can stop him with this."

"*CatOff*?"

Lucy unscrewed the cap and squirted some orange-colored gel into her palm. She pushed it under Bonnington's nose. Bonnington reeled back as if he'd been punched. With a hiss of indignation he jumped off the chair and dipped out through his cat door again.

"It smells like oranges," Lucy explained. "He hates

oranges. Mom puts this near the roses so Bonnington won't poop there."

David took the bottle and read the instructions. "Yeah, but if it works for Bonnington it might work for Conker. The last thing we want is *SquirrelOff* on the box. No, we'll just have to keep our fingers crossed that Bonnington doesn't go near it *and* that Conker comes our way — which he will, when he sees what I've got for him. Go and look in my coat pockets — and don't spill anything."

Lucy hurried away. She returned carrying a brown paper bag. "Acorns!" she gasped. "Where did you get them?"

"Never mind," said David. "I feel weird enough about stealing them as it is. Come on, it's time to lay the trail."

After a brief debate, they decided to set the trap behind the rock garden. David scrabbled over the crumbling stones and carefully placed the box out of sight. Then he took a handful of acorns and sowed them at intervals across the patch of ground between the rock garden and the brambles at the end of the garden. He saved most of the acorns for the box itself, tilting it slightly so the nuts rolled into the deepest corner. Finally, he took an unshelled peanut off the bird feeder and tied the string very tightly around it. "That's his 'treat,'" he told Lucy, leaving the bait just inside the hutch. He lifted the sliding door of the trap and wedged it open with the ball of clay. "That's it, we're ready."

Lucy, perched like a pixie in front of the rock garden, could hardly speak. "What now?"

"Now it's up to Conker," said David, wiping his hands on the front of his sweatshirt. He flicked an acorn cup into the stones. "All we can do is wait."

GOTCHA!

Lucy, being Lucy, *couldn't* wait. She checked the trap at least half a dozen times before her mom came home that afternoon. On each occasion, nothing had changed. Every nut was exactly as David had left it. The only visitor to the trap was a tiny spider, who, according to Lucy, didn't look strong enough to pull a cat hair, never mind a piece of string.

"You have to be patient," David told her, as the day wore on and darkness fell. "It's a trap, remember. He might be suspicious."

Lucy stuffed her hands into her jeans pockets. She peered sadly through the kitchen window, her worry reflected in the rain-spattered glass.

Liz came in then, cuddling Bonnington. "Come on, Lucy. Time for bed."

Lucy turned and walked out of the kitchen in silence.

"Oh dear," said Liz, putting Bonnington down. "I take it you had no luck with Conker?"

David gave a doleful shrug.

Liz tiptoed to the door and pushed it shut. "Never mind. She'll cheer up when she sees what I bought her this afternoon." She opened a cabinet and took an old cake pan off the top shelf. Inside was a small brown box. She handed it to David. "It's her birthday next week. Take a look."

"Birthday?"

"Sssh," Liz said nervously. "She's got ears like an elephant."

David flipped the box open. "Nice," he smiled, sliding a camera out of the wrapping.

Liz put a finger against her lips. "Do you think it's all right for an eleven-year-old? You know a little about cameras, don't you?"

"Hmm," went David, panning around the room. "This'll be fine. All she has to do is point and —"

Snap!

"Oh, David. Don't waste the film," Liz chided. The camera lens was pointing straight at her.

"Never touched it. Honest." He waggled a finger above the shutter.

Liz frowned and turned to the window. "Must have been something in the garden, then. I definitely heard a snapping sound."

David swung to his feet. "A snap? Not a clank?"

"A snap," said Liz. "Why, what's the matter?"

David backed away down the hall. "Don't say *a word* to Lucy. I think it's Mr. Bacon's trap."

He ran next door and rang the bell.

As usual, Henry looked irked to see him. "What now, boy? I'm watching the news."

"Your trap, Mr. Bacon. I think it worked!"

Henry nearly leapt out of his slippers. "Back gate," he hissed and closed the door. David hurried down the side of the house. Mr. Bacon unbolted the gate. David followed him into the garden. As they passed the kitchen Mr. Bacon reached in and threw a switch. A string of ornamental lamps came on, lighting up the lawn like an airport runway. At the end of the runway was the dreaded trap.

Its door was closed.

"Gotcha!" Henry hooted, doing a jig. He dropped to his knees, took a flashlight from his pocket and shone it fervently through the mesh.

David's heart skipped a very large beat. He was wondering what sort of jail term he'd get if he knocked Henry out, stole the trap and made off with Conker, when suddenly Mr. Bacon slapped a hand on the grass.

"Drat. False alarm. Caught a hog instead."

David knelt down and took a quick look. To his relief, a young hedgehog was shuffling around in the box, nibbling away at the lump of cheese.

"Where'd that thing come from?" Henry grumbled.

"Probably lives here," said David. "It is allowed."

"Do you want it?" Henry snapped.

David gave him a withering look. "What am *I* going to do with a baby hedgehog? Come on, Henry, let it go."

Muttering about his lame knee, Mr. Bacon lifted the trap and carried it to the end of the garden. There, under David's watchful eye, he let the hedgehog roll to freedom.

"Have to place the trap higher," he mumbled, looking around for a suitable spot as they filed back onto the lawn again.

"Hmm," went David, miles away. But as the gist of Henry's statement sank in, he quickly saw a chance to do Conker a favor. "Yes! That's a GREAT idea!"

Henry bumped to a halt.

"Be a terrible nuisance if you had to keep resetting the trap, wouldn't it? If you raised it off the ground, hedgehogs and . . . other things couldn't get in. Rats could, though, because they like to climb."

Henry tapped a foot. "Could put it above the flower pots, perhaps?" Near the kitchen window was a rack.

On the lowest shelf of three was a row of flower pots. The middle shelf was empty. It had to be a meter off the ground at least.

"Could dangle a rope bridge," Henry mused, "so Ratty can scramble up and think he's smart."

Fine, thought David. Put an exercise wheel in the corner if you like. *Just get it off the ground so Conker can't reach it.*

"Do it tomorrow," Mr. Bacon sniffed, dumping the trap on a pile of old junk near his garden shed.

"Great. I'll go, then," David said, back-pedaling triumphantly toward the gate. He clenched a fist and turned away — just as something went *clank* behind him. He paused and looked back at the pile of junk. An old metal watering can had slipped sideways across a bag of compost, knocking its spout against a stack of roof tiles.

David shrugged and reached for the gate latch. But as he lifted it, Gadzooks popped into his mind. The image of the dragon was so clear and so sudden that David dropped the latch as if it were aflame. The special dragon huffed what looked like a smoke ring. It seemed to contain a fragment of speech: . . . *hiding place, low to the ground* . . . David's stomach tightened. He turned and peered at the pile of junk.

"Lost your bearings?" Henry barked. He nodded at the gate.

"Just going," David muttered, deep in thought. He glanced again at the watering can. It was probably nothing. Wishful thinking. Hopeful imaginings.

Dragon dreaming.

He shut the gate behind himself and walked back home.

In the living room, Liz was watering plants. "So, any news?"

David kicked off his shoes and flopped out on the sofa. "Henry caught a hedgehog."

"I hope he let it go."

"'Course. I made him."

"Hmm," Liz grunted, looping her hair. She picked a dead leaf off a Christmas cactus. "So it works, the rodent remover?"

David squeezed a cushion against his stomach. "Yes, but Conker's safe — for now. I tricked Henry into raising the trap off the ground. But if he changes his mind and puts it back . . ."

Liz topped up the yucca plant's saucer and dabbed at a spill with a piece of tissue. "Talk to Gadzooks if you're worried," she said. "Special dragons can help at times like this."

David rolled his eyes to the ceiling. Sometimes he had to wonder about Liz. She always seemed like such a practical person and yet . . . "Why do you talk about the dragons as if they were real?"

"They are real," she said in a throwaway voice. "To me and Lucy, anyway."

David let his shoulders sag. "I think I'd be better off chatting with Bonnington."

"Oh, no," said Liz with a serious frown. "He's as dumb as a halibut is wide. Gadzooks can reach you on . . . a deeper level."

David threw her a quizzical look.

"You said yourself, he suggested Snigger's name. You asked him a question and he spoke to you, didn't he?"

"That was different," David muttered, looking away. Even so, he thought about the flash of Gadzooks in Henry's garden. Had the dragon been trying to speak to him then? No, it was ridiculous. How could a pottery dragon have any idea where Conker might be hiding? "Anyway," he said, "while we're on the subject of peculiar things: I keep hearing a noise, in bed, at night."

"Noise?" said Liz, tending the leaves of a spider plant.

David pointed upward. "From the Dragons' Den. It sounds like a purr, but it's not — it's a *hurr*."

"Oh, I wouldn't worry about that," said Liz, touching the snout of the dragon by the yucca plant, "that's just . . . the central heating. Feet off the sofa, please." She whacked his ankles and swept out of the room.

David swung his feet to the floor. For a moment or two he sat in silence, twiddling his thumbs, staring into space. Then a strange thought crept into his mind. He glanced at the dragon by the yucca plant, then at all the walls of the living room in turn. "Liz," he called out, "there aren't any radiators!"

You don't *have* any central heating, he thought.

SIGHTING

He decided it was one of Liz's jokes. There was a gas fire on the chimney wall. As yet, he had never seen it working. What he was expected to believe, no doubt, was that fire-breathing dragons kept the house nice and toasty and were a cheaper alternative to electricity or gas.

Yes, Liz. Very funny. Ha, ha.

Dragons. The spiky little whatsits were popping up everywhere. David often saw Lucy carrying them around. She would leave one on the mantelpiece, or take one off the mantelpiece, or move them bafflingly around the living room. In the last few days, when the weather forecasts had hinted at frost, a couple had even appeared in the picture window near the top of the stairs. To anyone outside the Pennykettle household it would have seemed . . . eccentric, to put it mildly. David had simply learned to live with it.

Still, whichever way the house was heated, the tenant was glad for the warmth the next day. It was Sunday and the heavens had opened. It rained so heavily that even Lucy was forced to admit that sensible squirrels would not venture out in such a downpour, much less investigate traps. She spent most of that day in the company of her mom, working on a drawing project for school. David, glad for the isolation, typed away at an essay for college. It was the quietest day he'd known since his arrival.

On Monday, however, everything changed. David woke to a blaze of sunlight streaming in through a chink in his curtains. He squinted at the clock. Quarter to eight. Pushing Bonnington onto the floor, he wandered, bleary-eyed, into the kitchen. Right away he caught sight of Lucy clambering into the back of the rock garden. He put an ear out for Liz but couldn't hear her anywhere. He knocked quietly but urgently on the kitchen window. Lucy turned so fast she lost her footing, causing a mini-avalanche of stones. She scowled at the tenant and formed the word, "What?" David beckoned her in.

"What are you doing?"

"Checking the trap."

"I know *that*. Don't you think your mom'll be a tad suspicious if she sees you playing Queen of the Castle?"

"She's in the shower," said Lucy, looking David up and down. "Is that what you wear to bed?"

The tenant was dressed in fluffy blue socks, brown pajama bottoms, and a T-shirt with a picture of a large yellow duck. "What's wrong with it?" he said.

The doorbell rang before Lucy could tell him. "I'll go," she said, swinging down the hall. "We don't want to *scare* people away."

"Charming," David muttered, and rattled some cornflakes into a dish.

He was reaching for the milk when the front door opened and he heard Lucy say, "Oh, it's you."

"Haven't got long," Mr. Bacon boomed. "Step aside, child. Where's the boy?"

David closed the fridge and went to investigate. "What's up, Henry? I'm having my breakfast."

Mr. Bacon held up a tuft of gray fur.

Lucy gasped and stumbled back against the stairs.

David felt his stomach sink into his socks. "W-where did you find that?"

"Snagged on a corner of my window box," said Henry. "Think you need a good pair of goggles, boy. That rat you saw belongs up a tree."

"You leave him alone!" Lucy cried, stomping forward.

David intercepted fast. "Calm down," he hissed, pulling her aside. "He didn't say he *caught* anything, did he?"

Lucy's eyebrows knotted together. David turned to Mr. Bacon again. Choosing his words very carefully he asked, "Are you saying you've seen a *squirrel?*"

"Couldn't miss it," Henry rapped. "Sitting on my windowsill, clear as a nut. Practically knocking on the glass, it was. Nearly spilled my coffee down my pants with the shock."

"You should have!" snapped Lucy.

David turned on her again. "Lucy, will you let *me* deal with this?"

Lucy folded her arms and huffed.

David floated a hand about chest height. "So, it was . . . well off the ground, you mean?"

Mr. Bacon's mustache wiggled with impatience. "Should I draw you a diagram, boy?"

"I'm not sure," said David, scratching his head. *How could Conker get onto a windowsill?* "This squirrel, how many eyes did it have?"

"Is this a joke?!" barked Henry. "Two, you fool."

"Two?" gasped Lucy.

Mr. Bacon leaned down to her height. "One on either side of its ratty little nose."

That was one gibe too many for Lucy. With a rush of vehemence she kicked the door hard, slamming it shut in Henry's face.

David emitted a horrified squeak. "Lucy! What are

you doing?" He yanked the door open. Mr. Bacon was holding a hankie to his nose. "Sorry, Mr. Bacon. Wind blew it shut. Back door. Just a draft. Happens all the time." He gave a jovial smile and stepped onto the porch, guiding Henry down the path. "So, it was a squirrel all along? Well, well. Easy mistake to make at a distance. Still, now that we know there isn't a rat, you won't need to bother with the trap — will you?"

Mr. Bacon stood to one side. "Squirrels are the scourge of the garden, boy. Sooner we snare the beast, the better." And with that he turned crisply on his heels, marched across the drive and got into his car.

David said a swear word under his breath. He turned back to the house. Lucy was tapping her foot against the step. "Let *me* deal with this," she toadied, and slammed the door on David as well.

Sputtering furiously, he flipped the mail slot open. "Lucy, let me in. It's freezing out here."

"Don't care. I wish you never came."

"Right now, so do I. Open up, we've got to talk. That wasn't Conker on the windowsill."

"Yes, it was."

"No, it wasn't. A one-eyed squirrel couldn't jump up there. There must be another squirrel in the garden."

"It was Conker!"

David banged the mail slot shut. He opened it again with a fresh argument. "All right, if it *was* Conker, that means his injury must have healed. Now, let me in — or I'll ring the bell until your mom comes down."

"Don't bother, she's already here," said a voice.

The door swung open. Liz was holding Lucy by the shoulders like a hostage. She looked as if she were about to explode. "What's going on?"

David ran in, rubbing his arms. "Henry saw a squirrel."

"It was Conker," cried Lucy. "And Mr. Bacon's going to try *extra* hard to catch him! And it's all *his* fault!" She stabbed a toe at David's shins.

"OK, I've had enough of this," said Liz, pushing Lucy toward the stairs. "Bedroom, until it's time for school. As for you . . . ," she turned on David, ". . . is that really what you wear to bed?"

David snorted in annoyance and retreated to his room.

"That's it," he said to Bonnington, lobbing the cat off the bed. "That trap has got to go. If she's this bad when Henry doesn't catch a squirrel, what's she going to be like if he does?!"

M-yew, went Bonnington, arching his back. He shook himself and padded across the room to the chair where David dumped his clothes overnight. A sweater had fallen on the floor. Bonnington took a few sniffs of the wool, pawed it and pushed his nose under the hem.

"Gotta think of a way to get rid of it," said David. "Something permanent, that even Liz will approve of."

A muffled meow broke into his thoughts.

Bonnington had snuggled inside the sweater. The fabric bulged like soup on simmer as the cat decided to fight it for fun.

David groaned and scooped the bundle up into his arms. Bonnington's head popped out of the neck. "What are you doing?" David asked him.

Meow? went Bonnington.

"That's my favorite sweater, cat. You're going to pull the threads if you get yourself st —"

David sat back and blinked.

Meow? went Bonnington again.

A sly smile crept across the tenant's face. "Yes-ss, you'll help me save Conker, won't you?"

A-row? went Bonnington as if he could look into the tenant's mind and didn't quite like the picture he was seeing.

"Trust me," David whispered. "Won't hurt a bit. By dinnertime tonight, you are going to be a real hero. . . ."

BONNINGTON DISAPPEARS

Around four that afternoon, Liz and Lucy arrived home from school and found David in the kitchen, washing dishes.

"Goodness, I must be dreaming," said Liz. "I see washed pots and a tidy table and . . . is that a freshly mopped floor?"

David shuffled with embarrassment. "Had a little mud on my sneakers and . . ."

"Don't spoil it," said Liz, raising her hands. "You cleaned up. That's what matters. How come you're home so early?"

David clicked his tongue. "Erm, lecture was canceled. There's tea in the pot."

Liz glanced at the cat-shaped cozy and the three

clean mugs waiting to be filled. "Gosh, now I do feel pampered." She smiled and went to hang up her coat.

Lucy passed her in the doorway. "Have you checked?" she whispered, running to the window.

"Yes. No sign. We're talking again, I guess?"

"Mom says I have to. Have you *really* checked?"

"Lucy —"

"Okay, let's try this tea." Liz breezed in, pushing back her sleeves. She sat at the table and started to pour.

"Oh, I almost forgot," said David, "I put some *Chunky Chunks* out for Bonnington but he doesn't . . . erm . . . seem to be around."

Lucy glanced at the empty basket. "Did you rattle his food?"

David shook his head.

Lucy sighed at the tenant's hopelessness. "I'll find him," she said, and walked out rattling some chicken-flavored cat treats.

Two minutes later she was back. Bonnington was nowhere to be found, she said.

"Did you check the kitchen closet?" asked Liz.

"Twice," said Lucy.

"Try the garden, then."

Lucy went out, rattling hard.

"Funny," said Liz. "It's very unusual for Bonny to go missing. I hope he didn't get himself in any sort of —"

A-row-oo-wee-yow-oooooo!

"That was him," she said, putting down her tea.

"Mom!" cried Lucy.

Liz dashed into the garden.

David said a quick prayer and shot out after her.

On the patio, Lucy explained what had happened. "I rattled the box and he yowled, Mom. Listen." She shook the box again.

Yow-oo-wee-ar-ooooo!

Liz twisted toward Mr. Bacon's garden. "That came from next door."

"Hhh!" gasped Lucy, nearly dropping the cat treats. "You don't think . . . ?"

Liz didn't wait to hear. With a face like thunder she

set off at high speed for Henry's front door, Lucy and David close behind.

As luck would have it, Henry had just arrived home from the library. He tipped his hat as Liz approached.

"Henry, let me into your garden now!" Liz pointed at the paneled gate.

"Problem, Mrs. P.?"

"Bonnington's in there. If he's stuck somewhere he shouldn't be, there's going to be trouble!"

Henry's face turned the color of an uncooked pancake. He jangled his keys and went into the house. He emerged seconds later from the kitchen door, and slid the bolt on the garden gate.

Liz and Lucy flashed down the path.

Within seconds, they heard a piercing scream. Every bird within a half-mile radius took to the air and flew for its life.

Mr. Bacon gasped in horror. His trap was on the ground, turned over on its side.

A furry face was peering through the mesh.

"Get him out!" Liz thundered, pointing at the box.

Henry raised a trembling hand to his mouth. "But it's impossible," he blustered. "That cat's too fat."

"I beg your pardon?"

Mr. Bacon bent like a tree in a gale. "Size to space ratio, Mrs. P. Scientific improbability. The cat must have practically stuffed itself in."

"I'll stuff *you* in," Liz said dangerously, "if you don't release my cat, right now."

Henry hooked a finger under his collar. He crouched down slowly and reached for the door. Bonnington hissed and bared his fangs. Mr. Bacon drew back in alarm.

"Let me," said David, kneeling down. Bonnington's reaction was no less virulent. He took one look at David and spat like water in a pan of hot oil. David leaned closer and gritted his teeth. "Cut it out," he whispered. "I came to let you out." He yanked the trap open. Bonnington sprang out. He took a hostile swipe at the tenant's hand, then dropped to his belly and tried to slink away. Lucy scooped him up and handed him to Liz. Bonnington pushed his nose inside her cardigan and started to mew like a day-old kitten.

"Okay," said Liz, almost nose to nose with Henry. "That trap has got to go."

Lucy's eyes widened. She shot a glance at David. He studied his nails and gave a tuneless whistle.

Henry Bacon sucked in through his teeth. "I'll definitely rethink it, Mrs. P. Minor modifications, perhaps."

"I'll minor modify you," Liz growled. "If that door had come down and trapped Bonnington's tail, he could have been seriously hurt." (Bonnington tentatively flicked his tail as if making sure he still possessed one.)

"But Mrs. P.," protested Henry, "what about the —?"

"Get rid of it, Henry, or else!" And ordering Lucy to come along with her, Liz turned sharply and marched back home.

Mr. Bacon looked to David for support.

"Want a hand smashing it up?" said the tenant.

BIRTHDAY IDEAS

When David returned to the kitchen, Bonnington was being treated like royalty. There was cream in his water bowl and salmon in a saucer. Lucy was hunkering nearby, stroking him. Liz was covering the *Chunky Chunks* with plastic wrap.

"Phoof," said David. "Thank goodness he's safe."

"Quiet," said Lucy. "You mustn't remind him. He has a delicate constipation, doesn't he, Mom?"

"Constitution," Liz corrected, washing her hands. "Yes, he's been through a horrible ordeal."

Lucy ran Bonnington's tail through her fingers and told him he'd been a very brave kitty.

"A real hero, isn't he?" David said, reaching down to scratch Bonnington's ear.

Fzzzn-uffn-pffn-sass! Bonnington hissed.

"Goodness gracious!" Liz exclaimed. "That's twice in five minutes that he spat at you."

David did his best to give an innocent shrug. "I guess he's feeling a little fragile. Um, how long till dinner?"

"About an hour," said Liz, flicking a glance at a wide-eyed dragon on the windowsill. She frowned and threw the tenant a suspicious look.

David responded with a cheesy grin. "Think I'll go and lie low — I mean down — for a while. See you both later. Bye, Bonners."

With a hesitant wave, he retreated to his room and sank back against the door, sighing with relief. Aw, that had been close. Too close, really. If cats could talk instead of hiss . . .

Best not to think about it. Work. That was the thing to do now. Forget about rat traps. Catch up on the "canceled" lecture he'd missed. Grabbing a college book from his bag, he flopped onto the bed and got back to his studies. *A Hole at the Pole: The*

Disappearing Ozone Layer. For fifteen minutes his eyes scanned glorious, glacial pictures and skimmed over paragraphs of icy text. Distantly, he heard the thump of a hammer and the splintering sound of breaking wood. In the midst of this, the telephone rang. Shortly afterward, he heard muttered voices in the hall. The front door opened and closed. Seconds later, the *back* door opened and closed. David tossed the book aside. It was hopeless; he couldn't face college work now. The words were just merging into a meaningless mush. He put his head back and let his mind wander.

It settled on Lucy's birthday.

During the Sunday of heavy rain, he had secretly asked Liz what he might buy Lucy. *Don't be silly*, she'd laughed. *You don't have to bother.*

"No, I want to," he'd replied, knowing he'd feel awful if he didn't do something.

The trouble was, what?

He took his wallet from his jeans and opened it wide. A cavernous gap yawned back. His mind leapt forward in time. *Happy Birthday, Lucy. Here's a postage stamp. It's all I could afford. Send someone a letter!* He snapped the wallet shut and lobbed it at his desk. It hit the mouse, making the computer screen clear. A few paragraphs of double-spaced text appeared: the beginning of an essay he'd been typing earlier.

Might as well continue with that, he thought — when suddenly an idea popped into his head. An idea that would really make Lucy's day.

What if he *did* try writing her a story?

It couldn't be that difficult, could it? A little tale about squirrels? A short animal adventure? He already had the characters and setting: Conker, Cherrylea and the bullying Birchwood chasing around the library gardens? He could type it, print it, bind it at college — make it look like a real book. A special present from David and Gadzooks. It was worth a try.

It was also cheap.

"What do you think?" he said, swinging up into a sitting position and taking Gadzooks off the windowsill.

He ran a finger over the dragon's snout. "We need an angle. A plot, I s'pose."

He closed his eyes briefly to think.

And, in that blink, it happened again. David saw Gadzooks take his pencil from his mouth and scribble down another word on his pad:

Nutbeast

"Nutbeast?" David muttered. "What's that supposed to mean?"

There was a gentle *hrring* noise from above.

Suddenly, David's door burst open and Lucy skidded in, panting for breath. Her face was as white as a piece of fish.

"What's the matter?" David asked, putting Gadzooks down gently on his desk.

"You've got to come," Lucy gulped. "He's here. We've got him."

It took a few seconds for her words to sink in. "The trap? You mean it worked?"

Lucy danced on her toes. "He's in the box and he's eating the nuts."

David jumped up and peered through the window. "You looked? It's definitely Conker?"

Lucy bit her lip. "Not exactly."

David threw her a critical stare.

"It's got two eyes and a great big smile."

"*What?*" said the tenant, color draining from his face.

"It's Snigger," said Lucy. "We caught Snigger in the box."

THE WRONG SQUIRREL

Don't be ridiculous," David said, poking his head around the door of his room and glancing furtively into the kitchen.

"It's true," said Lucy. "Can we tell Mom?"

"Absolutely not. Where is she, anyway?"

"Went to see a man about a dog."

"*What?*"

"She hasn't really. It's what she says when she's buying me presents. I'll be eleven at the end of next week, you know."

"I know," muttered David, hurrying down the hall.

"Oh, good," said Lucy, skipping along behind him, "will you go to see the dog man, too?"

"I'm going to see this smiling squirrel, first."

"It's great, isn't it — Snigger coming?"

David paused at the kitchen door. "It's *not* Snigger. It can't be Snigger. Snigger is running around the library gardens." He yanked the door open and went dashing out.

Lucy stood still and pondered for a moment. "I don't think he is," she said earnestly.

But the tenant was too far away to hear.

When Lucy caught up with him, David was sprawling flat across the rock garden, peeking at the box on the other side. He waved at Lucy to be quiet as she crawled up beside him. Cocking their heads, they listened to the sound of acorn shells being cracked and scattered on the bottom of the box.

"Let's move the trap out and take a better look," said David.

He stood up and scrambled over the rock garden. A few loose stones crumbled out of the earth and pitter-pattered into the side of the hutch. The acorn cracking instantly stopped. David hauled the box into the open.

The captured squirrel chattered loudly and hid itself in the darkest corner.

"We're not going to hurt you," Lucy tried to tell it as David carried the trap across the lawn. He set it on the bench near Lucy's swing.

"I'll see if I can coax him into view," he said. He crouched down quietly and scratched the mesh. "Stay back, Luce, they can bite, you know. You'd have to go to the hospital if he bit your — waargh!" Without warning, the tenant toppled backwards onto the grass.

"Hhh!" went Lucy, clapping her hands across her nose and mouth. The captured squirrel was clinging to the mesh with his feet splayed out and only his furry white tummy showing.

"Awesome!" she exclaimed.

"Glad you think so," David whined, checking his finger for signs of a scratch.

"That was a good trick," Lucy said.

"It was not a trick," David said curtly. "He jumped so fast I —" Then it occurred to him that Lucy wasn't talking to him at all; she was chatting to the squirrel.

"Did you come on your own?" David heard her ask. She had her head near the mesh now, blocking his view. "Was it you on Mr. Bacon's windowsill?"

"Lucy, don't get too close," said David. "That squirrel is very —" He froze mid-sentence as Lucy turned around. The captive squirrel was sitting forward, clamping its chisellike teeth around the mesh. It looked at Lucy and chirruped something; then squinted at David and flagged its tail. It twitched its whiskers, tilted its head, sat up proudly on its haunches — and *smiled*.

"I don't believe it," David gasped.

"Told you," smiled Lucy.

"But it *can't* be Snigger. Why would Snigger come here?"

Lucy seemed to think the answer was obvious. "To help Conker, of course."

David gave her a withering look. "Lucy, don't be silly. How is *he* going to know about Conker?" The tenant sighed and rocked back on his heels. "What a shame. We were so close. Come on, you can do the honors."

Lucy stepped back, looking puzzled.

"Lucy, whoever he is, he's the wrong squirrel, isn't he? We can't keep him imprisoned. We have to let him go."

Lucy squeezed her fingers into fists. She wasn't about to give up yet. "Where's Conker?" she whispered, hunkering by the hutch. "Will you find him for me? It's very important."

The squirrel chirruped and turned in a little circle.

David sighed again but didn't interrupt. In a moment or two, the trap would be open and "Snigger" would be loose in the neighborhood once more.

"He's only got one eye," Lucy went on. The squirrel chattered something and flagged its tail. "Yes," said Lucy, "horrible, isn't it? Tell him we want to catch him, to help him."

"*Chuk,*" went the squirrel.

Lucy turned to David. "I think he's going to help."

"Great," said the tenant. "Open the door."

Lucy raised the panel.

Faster than a fish down Bonnington's throat, the squirrel was out. Like a gray leaf tumbling in a blustery gale, it hopped and bounced across the Pennykettles' lawn.

"He's going through the fence to Mr. Bacon's!" yelled Lucy.

"No, he isn't," said David, watching the squirrel closely. "He's coming back toward the garden shed."

"No," said Lucy, "the terracotta pots."

"No, look." David pointed. "He's running along the patio. He's . . ."

"*Oh no!*" they shouted together.

The runaway squirrel had just shot into the house.

SQUIRREL IN
THE HOUSE

Come on!" yelled David, bounding up the garden, "we've got to get him out before he does any damage!"

Lucy squealed: "What if Bonnington gets him?"

"What if *he* gets *Bonnington*, more like it?"

Oddly enough, at that very moment, Bonnington was lapping water from his dish. He was so absorbed in his afternoon drink that he didn't see the squirrel run into the kitchen, jump up on the table, hop along the counters, sniff at the fruit bowl, scramble down the ironing board and whizz off up the hall. But a few seconds later when David skidded in, tipping over a chair, spilling a box of cornflakes, standing in the litter box and kicking *Chunky Chunks* across the kitchen floor, the big brown tabby did the sensible thing. He slinked into his box and stayed put.

"Have you got him?" panted Lucy, winging around the door.

"Up here!" came a yell from somewhere near the stairs.

Lucy rushed through, in time to see the squirrel come scampering down the banister. "Hhh!" she gasped as he leapt onto a lampshade, swung for a moment, dropped to the carpet and bolted through her legs.

"Your room!" she cried. "He went into your room!"

David flashed past her and flung the door open wide. "Are you sure?" Everything seemed remarkably still.

"There," Lucy whispered, pointing to the book-shelves.

On the third shelf up sat the bushy-tailed intruder. He was eating a chocolate bar with nuts.

David reached for an empty cardboard box. "Shut the door. I'm going to grab him."

Lucy looked doubtful. "He's pretty quick."

The tenant tapped the side of his nose. "I'll teach him to steal my chocolate." He got onto his toes and stalked across the room.

The squirrel wasn't impressed. At the first hint of cardboard moving toward it, it skipped off the bookshelf, bounced sure-footed off a gooseneck lamp, sped across the mantelpiece (launching the space shuttle into unexpected flight) and hopped calmly onto the desk. David pursued it, slamming the box against the chimney wall, but always a bounce behind. Twice he missed it, three times, four. Then he reached the alcove space — and disaster.

"Waar!" he cried, tumbling forward and ending up in a crumpled heap on the floor.

The squirrel chewed the corner of David's mouse pad, then leapt onto the windowsill and paused by Gadzooks.

"Look!" cried Lucy.

David dragged the cardboard box off his head.

The squirrel was sniffing at Gadzooks. And it was surely a trick of the afternoon light but . . . did the dragon just *wink* at the squirrel? David batted the box away. The sudden clatter made the squirrel leap around. It flagged its tail, chirruped at Gadzooks, smiled at Lucy and shot out of the window.

Lucy sprinted across the room and watched the squirrel depart across the lawn. "Don't forget about Conker!" she shouted.

"Aw," groaned David. "Thank goodness that's over."

But it wasn't, not quite.

By the door, a foot was tap-tap-tapping.

David and Lucy looked around.

"OK," said Liz, with her arms tightly folded, "which of you would like to start?"

· PART TWO ·

THE FIRE WITHIN

A VERY
SPECIAL PRESENT

Get away from that door," Liz said brusquely. "I told you twice. Don't make me say it again."

Lucy stuffed her hands into the pockets of her jeans. "What's he doing?" she said with a sniff.

"Typing, from the sound of it."

"I know," she complained. "It's *all* he does now." She flopped back against the tenant's door in a huff.

"He's working," said Liz, taking the cake from the fridge, "which is what you're supposed to be doing, remember? Come on, give me a hand with the table."

Lucy moped into the kitchen. She gripped the end of the kitchen table while her mom pulled out the extending piece. "Tablecloth," said Liz. "The pretty one, please."

Lucy yanked it out of a drawer. "It's your fault for being so hard on him."

"We can't have squirrels running riot in the house."

"It was only some cat litter on the *floor*."

Liz took the tablecloth and flicked it out. "And a secret trap. And plants uprooted all over the rock garden. Not to mention that unspeakable business with Bonnington. He's lucky he got off as lightly as he did. If he were your age, he'd have been sent to his room for a week."

"Mom, he's *been* in his room for a week!"

"Well, at least it kept you both out of mischief, didn't it?"

Lucy sighed and pushed a finger back and forth across the counter. "Didn't you *know* he was setting the trap?" She glanced past her mother to a pretty little dragon perched on top of the microwave oven. It had ears like seashells and eyes like moons.

Liz opened a cabinet and took out some dishes. "It doesn't matter what I know. What's done is done. Put these out — with dessert spoons, please."

Lucy took the dishes and plunked them down haphazardly around the table. Bonnington, sitting statuesquely on a stool, winced with every place that was "set." "I bet he forgot my story," Lucy grumbled. "He promised he'd read me one for my birthday."

"Lucy, he's twenty years old," Liz said. "He doesn't want to be pestered by a ten-year-old child."

"Eleven," Lucy said, indignantly. "I'm nearly grown up."

"Well, act like it then," her mother trumped her. "Learn a little patience. You never know what might be around the corner."

At that moment, David's door creaked open and the tenant strolled buoyantly into the kitchen. "Party time," he smiled, trying to scoop a smidgen of frosting off the cake. Liz smacked his knuckles with a wooden spoon. "Ow," said the tenant, and tousled Lucy's hair. "How's the birthday girl?"

"There aren't enough spoons," Lucy said haughtily. "I'm going to get some more from the front." She waltzed out with a mighty sniff.

Liz and David exchanged a little eyebrow traffic.

"A little frosty there," he said.

"Hmm," said Liz, glancing down the hall. "This story you're typing had better be worth it. She genuinely thinks you gave her the brush-off."

David let out a sneaky laugh. "Just keep her wondering for now. She'll be gobsmacked when she knows what I've really been doing. It might not be the greatest story in the world, but it's the thought that counts — I hope."

"She'll be thrilled," said Liz, reaching into the fridge. "Will you finish it today? I can't wait to hear it."

David shook his head. "Done the beginning and some of the middle, but I haven't even thought about the ending yet." He took a grape from a bowl of fruit salad and popped it into the corner of his mouth. "I'll ask Gadzooks when it's closer to the time. He's very good for inspiration, your dragon."

"*Your* dragon," Liz said, shaking a gelatin ring out of its mold. "Whatever magic he brings belongs to you."

Meow, went Bonnington, treading his paws.

David threw him a cat treat. Bonnington batted it across the kitchen, then dropped to the floor in hot pursuit. "Writing the story does feel a little magical. Sometimes I get so lost in the plot I find myself forgetting which parts are imagined and which are the parts that have actually happened."

"Or which parts have gone under the dishwasher," Liz sighed. She frowned as Bonnington tried, unsuccessfully, to squeeze his pink nose under the machine.

"It's a little like being on a mystery tour," said David, rescuing the treat with the blade of a knife. He washed off the fluff and returned it to Bonnington. "You sort of know you're going somewhere but you can't be sure where until you arrive. Does that make sense?"

"Very literary," said Liz. "Tell me, will the story have a happy ending?"

David shrugged and snitched another grape. "Like I said, haven't thought about it yet. Why? Is Lucy easily upset?"

Liz ran her hands down the front of her apron. "To be honest, I wasn't really thinking of Lucy."

David gave her an inquisitive look.

"Me," she said, flushing gently. "I get teary at the slightest thing. Last year we watched *Bambi* for Lucy's birthday. I was crying from start to finish. Very embarrassing."

"Mom, which spoons?" a snappy voice called.

"There are only a few good ones!" Liz bellowed in reply. She took off her apron. "Better go and help."

She blew a little kiss to the dragon on the fridge and puttered off down the hall.

David turned and looked thoughtfully at Bonnington. "She's doing it again, isn't she?" he whispered. "She doesn't mean *herself* at all. She's trying to tell me I shouldn't upset the dragons."

A-row, went Bonnington, whose only concern was another treat.

David scooped up a glob of frosting and dabbed a smidgen on Bonnington's nose. "Rule number 97,

Bonners. You shouldn't ever make a dragon cry." He smiled and let the cat lick his fingers. "Your humans are totally weird," he said.

Despite her moodiness earlier in the day, Lucy enjoyed her birthday party. As her friends trooped in one by one, she took great pride in introducing them to David. For the moment, it seemed, the rift was healed.

There was lots of food and games and presents. Christopher Jefferson, the boy who Lucy sat next to at school, brought her a book called *Martin's Mice*, which he claimed he'd read a hundred times *at least*. Beverley Sherbon gave her a bunny rabbit backpack and a plastic lobster with luminescent eyes. Samantha Healey gave her a jigsaw puzzle in a tin and some sparkling tubes of glitter paint. Lucy dabbed it on her arms and face (her mom said she looked like a piece of tinsel).

David, of course, had not forgotten her. He made a royal show of presenting Liz's daughter with a "Lucy" hat he'd found in a thrift shop. It had a green velvet bow with deep blue sequins. It was far too big, and kept slipping down over its namesake's eyes. But Lucy wore it all day long and bluntly refused to take it off.

The last presents she opened were the ones from her mom. When she unwrapped the little camera she jumped with joy and gave Liz a huge hug. Then she took pictures of *everything*: her friends spilling food and pulling faces; David in a party hat with Pixy Stix up his nose; Bonnington on the counter, finishing off the cake; her mom shooing Bonnington down. At five, when everyone was saying good-bye, Lucy was as happy as she'd ever been.

That was when the tenant winked at Liz and quietly slipped away to his room.

"Lucy," said Liz, recognizing the signal, "go and wash your face and hands now, all right?"

Lucy adjusted her Lucy hat and skipped upstairs without any argument.

She returned to find David and Liz in the living room. They were sitting at opposite ends of the sofa.

Lucy plunked herself down between them. It was then that she noticed a chair in the bay. It was facing the sofa, all trimmed with balloons and paper chains. Lucy looked at her mom. "Why does that chair have decorations on it?"

"I don't know," said Liz. "You'd better go and see."

Lucy hurried over. A note was lying on the seat. "STORYTELLER'S CHAIR," she read out loud.

David stood up and walked across the room.

Lucy's face lit up with delight. "Are you going to tell me a story?"

David took a sheaf of papers off the footstool. "No, I'm going to read you one."

Liz patted a cushion. "Lucy, over here."

Lucy sprinted over and bounced into place. David sat in the storyteller's chair.

"This is David's special present," said Liz. "You shouldn't interrupt until the end of a chapter."

"But doesn't he have a book?"

"Yes, he does," said David, shuffling the papers. "I typed one myself."

Lucy's mouth fell open in shock. "You *wrote* me a story?"

David nodded. "This is just the first few chapters, unfortunately. You'll probably have to wait until Christmas for the rest. Would you like to see what it's called?"

SNIGGER and the NUTBEAST
a squirrel story

for Lucy Pennykettle
(age 11 today)

Lucy gave an ecstatic nod. David turned the manuscript around and showed her.

"Sit back, be good and listen," said Liz.

Lucy sat back, as tame as one of Martin's mice. But she couldn't resist whispering, "What's a nutbeast?"

"Ah," said the tenant, "you'll have to wait and see."

And with that he turned the page and started to read.

THE TRUTH ABOUT THE NUTBEAST

Chapter One," said David. "The Nutfall That Wasn't."

"The nutfall that wasn't?" Lucy repeated, already interrupting.

"Oh, *Lucy*," her mother chided.

"It's all right," said David, raising a hand. "There's too much to read all at once, anyway. I'll have to do it in pieces." He leaned forward. "This is the opening line: *Once upon a time there was a squirrel called Snigger, who lived in the beech tree near the wishing fountain in the beautiful library gardens in Scrubbley.*"

"Aah," went Lucy, smiling at her mom.

"*One blustery morning*," David continued, "*Snigger was sitting on the fountain wall, enjoying his usual morning grooming, when another squirrel appeared at his side. It was Shooter —"*

Lucy turned to her mom. "Told you they went to the gardens," she whispered, then clamped a hand quickly across her mouth.

"— and judging by the way he came dashing up the hill, he clearly had his tail in a bit of a fluff. 'Snigger! Snigger! Come quickly!' he panted. 'Cherrylea says a nutbeast has come!'"

Bonnington looked warily over his shoulder.

"'A nutbeast has come?' Snigger repeated, doing a frenzied twirl on the wall.

'It was in the clearing by the oak tree!' gasped Shooter. 'It took our whole nutfall.'"

Lucy bit her lip and grabbed for a cushion. She squeezed it tightly onto her lap.

"We used to get a nutfall in the Crescent," said Liz. "Every autumn, before the oak was cut down, hundreds of acorns spilled across the road. It used to drive Mr. Bacon mad. When he went off to work in the mornings, they used to splinter and crack underneath his car. He said it cost a fortune in garage repairs."

"Mom," huffed Lucy, "we don't want to know about *Mr. Bacon*. We want to know what Snigger did next."

"He ran to the clearing with Shooter," said David, "and had the misfortune to bump into Birchwood."

"*'Watch it, fleabag!' Birchwood snarled. 'Or I'll pull your whiskers out and throw them in the pond!'*

'Not while I'm around!' cried a voice."

"Who was that?" asked Lucy, sitting up so quickly she disappeared inside her hat.

"Ringtail," said David. "He's Snigger's best friend. He came leaping to Snigger's defense. Before you could say 'fluff and whiskers', Ringtail and Birchwood were in a fight. They rolled and hissed and scratched and bit, each accusing the other of stealing the nutfall. It was a good thing Cherrylea came when she did or one of them could have been badly hurt.

"*'Stop!' she cried. 'I know what happened. There*

was a horrid black beast in the clearing last night. It was scuffling around in the fallen leaves, picking up as many nuts as it could find.'

"I bet it's that crow," said Lucy.

"What crow?" said Liz, looking confused.

"David saw one in the sycamore tree."

Bonnington twizzled an inquisitive ear.

"It was bigger than a crow," David said spookily. He turned another page. "Now, Ringtail, when he learned what had happened to the nutfall, decided to organize a nutbeast watch. Each of the squirrels took turns hiding in a yew tree and watching the oak at dusk that night. Guess who was watching when the nutbeast came back?"

"Snigger."

"Correct. He'd been sitting in the tree for absolutely ages, when all of a sudden something came plodding down the path." David lowered his voice to a whisper: *"Snigger's body turned as cold as ice. It was all he could do to prick his ears and concentrate on which way the thing was heading. First it shuffled along the path, kicking up little explosions of leaves. Then it was skidding down the earthy embankment, snapping twigs and stumbling against tree roots. It made strange, floppy, thudding sounds as it moved awkwardly into the clearing.*

"Suddenly, a chill wind howled across the gardens —"

"Hhh!" squealed Lucy. She covered her eyes and paddled her feet. Bonnington scooted off behind the television. Liz raised an eyebrow. David leaned forward.

"— and the branches of the yew tree parted! At last, Snigger saw the beast. It was just as Cherrylea had described: a great black shape, crouched low to the ground. Snigger watched with a sort of fascinated horror as it sifted through the leaf litter, hunting for acorns. Bravely, he crept along an outlying branch, hoping to get a closer look, when suddenly, without warning, the nutbeast reared! Snigger bolted for the

top of the yew. He sat there, panting in terror. But his fear was soon replaced by anger. For in that one daring glimpse he had learned the truth: the nutbeast was nothing more than . . . a man."

Lucy's mouth fell open in shock. "It was YOU!" she cried, jumping up. "You in your big black stinky coat! He's a robber, Mom. That's where he got those nuts for our trap. He stole them from the library gardens. That's why Snigger came to *our garden* — to see where the nutfall went!"

"Oh, David," Liz said, with a smile. "Is this true?"

"Chapter Two," he admitted. "It's all here; my complete confession — right up to the point where Snigger gets trapped in the box by mistake."

"I bet he went home to tell the others," scowled Lucy. "It wouldn't surprise *me* if Birchwood came around and bit your toe."

"Well, let's find out," said David, turning a page.

"Stop!" cried Lucy.

"What now?" her mom sighed.

"The dragons aren't here."

Liz rolled her eyes. "You can fetch Gawain and Gwendolen. But you'd better be quick — and we're *not* going to start again."

"Can Gadzooks come too?"

"He's on my windowsill," said David, meeting Lucy's eye.

Lucy whipped around and scooted to the door. "I might want to go to the bathroom as well."

"Oh, for goodness' sake," Liz sighed.

Lucy shot down the hall. Seconds later she returned with Gadzooks. She placed the special dragon on the coffee table, pushed her hat from her eyes and dashed out again.

After a pause Liz said, "You do realize you'll never be able to leave this house now? You'll be chained to your computer forever and a day writing squirrel stories for my daughter."

"It's your fault for giving him to me," said David.

Liz's gaze dipped lovingly to the pencil-chewing dragon. "Oh, he's always been with you. I just gave him shape, that's all."

Before David could comment, Lucy's voice came echoing down the stairs. "David! Quick! Come up here!"

"Oh, what's the matter with her now?" Liz sighed.

The answer was a gentle crash, followed by a squeal that seemed to rock the whole house.

Bonnington's eyes were wide with concern.

"Lucy?" Liz breathed, looking at the door.

David was up the stairs in a flash.

He found Lucy in the bathroom on her knees, in tears.

She was picking up the pieces of a broken dragon.

David sank down with a hand across his mouth. "Oh no," he gulped. "It's Gawain, isn't it?"

He put a comforting hand on Lucy's shoulder. The door banged open and Liz burst in. Her gasp of shock when she saw what had happened seemed to draw the heat right out of the room.

Lucy threw herself into her mother's arms. "I was coming to tell David and I tripped on the mat and he just fell, Mom. *Oh, I'm sorry!*"

"It's all right," Liz stuttered, swallowing hard, doing her best to stroke Lucy's hair. David noticed that her hands were shaking.

"Why were you shouting for me?" he asked Lucy quietly.

Lucy thrust an arm toward the window. "Mr. Bacon is trying to kill him."

David frowned and rose to his feet. He turned and peered out of the open window.

On the long green swath of Mr. Bacon's lawn, a strange confrontation was taking place. Mr. Bacon was scuttling around, spraying water from a garden hose. The object of his aim was a small, gray squirrel. It was darting energetically around his feet, trying to escape the crashing water. But, instead of dashing to the safety of a tree, it was running around in frightened circles.

Round and round and round it went.

As if it had lost all sense of direction.

As if it were completely blind in one eye.

IN MR. BACON'S GARDEN

It's Conker," said David, looking urgently at Liz.

"He came to drink in Mr. Bacon's pond," sobbed Lucy. "Mr. Bacon saw him and got very angry and started to shout and throw things at him."

"Sssh," Liz murmured, rocking her gently.

"I'll be back," David promised, glancing at Gawain. He ran a hand quickly over Lucy's head, hurdled over Bonnington and thundered downstairs.

Moments later he was hammering on Mr. Bacon's gate. "Mr. Bacon! It's David! Let me in!"

From the garden came a worrying cry of, "Gotcha!"

David grimaced and rattled the latch. The gate was firmly locked. There were roses growing above it as well, preventing any chance of him climbing over it. That left only one option. "Sorry, Mr. Bacon," David muttered to himself, stepping back a good ten paces, "no time for polite introductions..." He steadied himself, took a good deep breath, then went hurtling forward.

He was a yard from impact when Henry slipped the bolt and opened the gate. David sped through, shoulder first. He collided, painfully, with a barbecue grill, stumbled down the patio steps and belly-flopped onto the water-softened lawn.

"What in the heck are you doing?" barked Henry.

David winced with pain and flashed a glance around the garden. Conker seemed to have completely disappeared. "I saw you with a squirrel. Where did it go?"

"Sssh!" Henry raised a hand for silence. He cocked one ear toward his potting shed. "Rascals might be holed up in there."

"Rascals?" David queried, rubbing his knee. "You mean there was more than one?"

Mr. Bacon didn't reply. He tiptoed over to a small wheelbarrow and noiselessly picked out a long-handled fork. Without warning, he heaved the shed door open and dived inside as if charging into battle. "Yearrgghh!" he screamed, stabbing wildly. There was a thud and a *sproinng* and a cloud of dust, but nothing squirrellike emerged through the door. Either the squirrels weren't in the shed at all . . .

. . . or Mr. Bacon had managed to spear one.

David hobbled over as quickly as he could. To his relief he found the fork wedged safely in a bag of compost and Mr. Bacon sitting spread-eagle on the floor. A plastic plant pot rolled off a shelf and bounced with a clunk off Henry's head.

Mr. Bacon roared in annoyance. He leapt to his feet and stomped into the garden.

"Tricky little pests have to be here somewhere."

David took a peek behind Henry's trash can. There was nothing but wet leaves, wood lice and a potato chip bag. "Didn't you see which way they went?"

"Lost them while you were knocking," Henry muttered. "Could be anywhere. Pesky vermin."

"What's wrong with them, Henry?" David said hotly. "Most people think squirrels are cute."

Mr. Bacon's eye began to twitch. "Tree rats dig up the garden, boy. Worse than moles for holes, they are. Thought I'd seen them go away for good."

David's eyebrows came together in a look of deep suspicion. "What do you mean, you'd 'seen them go away'?"

"Oak," hissed Henry, flipping a switch on the side of the mower. He gave the engine cord a tug. The engine spluttered, but failed to start. "Out in the Crescent. Massive monstrosity. Friends in high places. Soon finished it off. Industrial chain saw. Barely left a twig."

David felt a tingle of coldness in his spine. "*You* cut the tree down?"

"Public service," Mr. Bacon sniffed.

David reeled back, fizzing with anger. "You made Conker homeless," he spluttered.

"Conker?" Mr. Bacon rattled. "What are you gibbering on about, boy?" He reached down to pull at the mower cord again. David plunked a foot on the engine and stopped him.

"Mr. Bacon," he said, in a very low voice, "did *you* hurt Conker's eye?"

"Are you drunk?" Mr. Bacon said, rather rudely. "Get your hoof off my mower before I call the cops." He shoved David aside and gave the mower cord a tug. At last the engine exploded into life — and so did something else.

"Waah!" yelped Henry, as a slim gray shape leapt out of the grass catcher and catapulted through his legs.

"I'll get it!" David cried and launched himself forward, only to stumble on the garden hose and stomp on Mr. Bacon's toe as he fell.

"Ow!" shouted Henry, hopping around, giving the mower a nudge in the process.

There was an ominous click. The mower shuddered — then set off, unattended, down the lawn.

"Oh no!" gasped David. "It's heading for the pond!"

But that was the least of his worries. The mower had barely rolled five meters when a second squirrel emerged from the grass catcher. It scrambled onto the engine housing, riding along like a little gray pirate. Even from a distance David could tell that the squirrel had one eye tightly closed.

Conker flagged his tail in distress. He hopped left, then right, then turned a full circle — too afraid or confused to leap to safety.

All the while the mower chugged on, and the water came closer and closer and closer.

"Stop that mower!" Mr. Bacon squawked.

David jumped to his feet. "I'll never catch it in time." But just as he was fearing a horrible accident, something very peculiar happened. Amazingly, the first squirrel ran out of hiding and hurtled toward the runaway machine. With a single bound it boarded the mower and knocked Conker straight off the engine housing. Conker tumbled onto the grass. He picked himself up and scurried out of sight. Meanwhile, the mower continued on course. It descended a lightly graveled slope, making an utterly awful racket as its blades churned up and spat out the stones. There was a *sploop* and a strange sort of bubbling sound. The mower lurched sideways and puttered to a stop. A wisp of smoke snaked up into the sky. Mr. Bacon made a sort of mewing sound.

To David's relief, the rescuing squirrel popped up on a boulder at the edge of the pond.

Mr. Bacon threw a rubber boot at its head. It missed and hit a garden gnome.

"Henry, leave it be," hissed David, pacing stealthily toward the squirrel. It twitched when it saw the nut-beast coming and hopped onto the back of a small stone badger.

David raised his hands in peace. "It's all right, I'm not going to hurt you."

"Whack it with a spade while you have the chance," said Henry.

"Sssh!" hissed David. "You'll frighten it away." He

looked the little squirrel straight in the eye. It sat back and did its best to smile. "Snigger," David whispered, trying Lucy's favorite tactic of talking to the animal, "bring Conker to the nutbox. It's the only way I'll be able to help him."

"You're the one who needs help," Mr. Bacon snorted.

"Mr. Bacon, will you *please* —" David was about to say "shut up," when Snigger unexpectedly chirped with alarm and fled at high speed to the end of the garden.

"Drat," said Henry. "Lost the little pest."

David stepped back in confusion. "Something frightened him," he said, and looked over his shoulder. "Something like . . ."

On a fencepost between the neighboring gardens was a huge black crow. It was sitting tight with its shoulders hunched, fixing its beady-eyed glare on the men.

David felt his mouth turn slightly dry. Even Mr. Bacon looked a little wary. "Wouldn't tangle with that. Looks a bit mean, if you want my opinion."

David gave an uneasy nod. He rose up slowly. The crow's eyes followed. Its sharp claws tightened against its perch.

David took a sideways step. Was it his imagination or was the bird trying to stare him down? He shuddered and found himself thinking of dragons, half-hoping some fire-breathing champion would come. Not surprisingly, he fixed on Gadzooks. In his mind's eye he saw the special dragon hurriedly scribbling something on his pad:

Caractacus

David whispered the name to the wind. The crow immediately screeched its displeasure, spread its wings and took to the sky. It swooped straight over David's head, making a dreadful screeching sound as it climbed and banked toward the sycamore tree. And there, cradled in the uppermost branches, David spotted something he hadn't seen before: a large crow's nest — not far from the hole beneath the eaves where a squirrel had once made a drey in Liz's roof. The crow split the air with another loud screech, as if to warn anyone with ears to listen that *it* was most definitely King of the Castle. David nodded and made the connection.

"It was you," he breathed as the great bird landed and folded its wings. "Caractacus, the crow. You were the one who hurt Conker's eye. . . ."

THE LAST DRAGON
IN THE WORLD

A steady drizzle had begun to fall by the time David came back to Liz's garden. He closed the gate with a hasty bang and hurried, teeth chattering, across the patio. As he was passing the kitchen window a plaintive meowing brought him to a halt. Bonnington was sitting on the garden bench, glistening like a fiber-optic Christmas tree. He had his paws tucked neatly under his tummy and raindrops misting the ends of his fur. Beside him lay the rabbit hutch, untouched since the day that Snigger had sprung it.

David wandered over and knuckled the cat's ear. "What are you doing sitting here, in the rain?"

Bonnington rose and rubbed his cheek against the corner of the hutch. David, remembering his words by the pond, studied the trap with renewed determination. If Conker *could* somehow find his way to it, there might yet be a chance to save him. He looked into the kitchen. No sign of Liz — or Lucy. "Come on," he whispered softly to Bonnington. And he hauled the trap into his shivering arms, took it to the rock garden and reset the door.

While he was checking the acorn trail, he issued the cat some hopeful orders. "I want you to be a guard cat, Bonners. There's a big crow nesting in the sycamore tree. If you see it in the garden, chase it away. Don't hurt it. Just shoo it away, OK?"

Bonnington, who'd been sitting on a large, flat rock impassively treading his columnlike paws, pricked his ears and sat to attention.

"Very good," said David. "Very guardlike. Now, let's go and see how Lucy is, shall we?"

With that, he led the way back into the house, Bonnington trotting along at his heels. As they passed through the kitchen and into the hall, the mail slot rattled and a small white envelope fluttered to the mat.

David picked it up. On the front was a picture of an in-jured fox. On the back were several lines of writing:

SCRUBBLEY WILDLIFE HOSPITAL APPEAL

*Frankie the fox was hit by a car and left
at the roadside with a broken leg.
We need your support to continue
caring for animals like him.*

PLEASE GIVE GENEROUSLY

David left it on the hall shelf for Liz.

Guessing that Lucy and her mom were in the Dragons' Den, he started up the stairs to tell them what had happened next door with Conker. The house was unusually still. There was a strange, almost haunted atmosphere about it, as if everything had somehow frozen in time. David thought about Gawain right then and looked at the door to the pottery studio. It was closed. A sign was hanging from the polished brass knob:

KILNING IN PROGRESS
DO NOT ENTER

Kilning. The word shaped like a question in David's mind, though he knew exactly what it meant. A kiln was a name for a potter's oven. When a dragon was being made, it would be put into an oven for firing — so its clay would harden and its glaze would set. But the last time David had visited this room he remembered that the only thing missing . . . was an oven. How could Liz be kilning dragons if she didn't have anything to fire them in?

Puzzled, he pressed one ear to the door. A faint *hrring* echoed through the panels. That noise again. It was everywhere. The tenant stood back, rubbing his lip. There was something very odd going on in this house, and the answer to the mystery lay inside this room. But he couldn't just barge in, unannounced. If Liz was making delicate repairs to Gawain, she'd be furious if he ignored the notice.

So he raised a knuckle, to knock — just as Bonnington, weaving around his feet, yowled loudly enough to rattle the lid off a trash can.

"That's Bonny," said a voice: Liz, from inside Lucy's room.

That meant the den was empty.

Temptation pushed David toward the door. Sign or no sign, he was going inside. He quickly let his hand close around the handle — and instantly wished he hadn't.

The brass was scorching hot.

Stifling a yelp of pain, he flapped his hand and twisted away, colliding lightly with the stair post behind him.

"What on earth is that cat doing?"

There was a creak of boards. Gentle footsteps. David dropped down to the turn in the stairs, dipping his head beneath the level of the landing. He slipped lower as Lucy's door creaked open.

"In you come," he heard Liz say.

Bonnington padded along the landing.

"Is David there?" Lucy's voice rang out.

David closed his hands in prayer. If Liz looked over the banister now . . .

"Not that I can see," she said, and backtracked into Lucy's room, this time leaving the door ajar.

"Oh. I want to know about *Conker*."

"I'm sure David won't let him get hurt," said Liz. "Now, into bed, birthday girl. I want you to rest, while I look at Gawain."

Lucy gave out a sad little sniff. "You *can* fix him, can't you, Mom? Nothing horrible's going to happen, is it?"

David heard a creak of springs and guessed that Liz had settled on the bed.

"Lucy, his fire is within you, always. If you love him, how can it ever go out?"

Lucy sniffed again and blew her nose. "Tell me the story of his fire tear, please."

His what? thought David, glancing at the dragons in the picture window. Was he dreaming it or had their ears just pricked up?

"Oh Lucy, you know it inside out."

"It is my *birthday*, Mom."

There was a pause, time enough for David to adjust his position before Liz said, "All right, but just a minute — and only if you promise to go to sleep afterward."

"I promise."

"All right, then, close your eyes. You know what to do."

"I have to dream back."

"Way back," said Liz. "To a time when the special people lived. A time when dragons roamed the earth."

David instinctively closed his eyes. Immediately a picture formed in his mind of something akin to pre-historic times. He began to imagine a dust-baked plain, littered with rocks and sparse vegetation, a stream winding through rocky outcrops, a world alive with animal calls, the sun beating down from a pale blue sky.

Into the picture, Liz put a character: "In a cave on the side of a hill lives a girl. She has flowing red hair and pale green eyes."

"Guinevere," said Lucy. "I dream her, Mom."

David nodded. He pictured her easily, barefoot in a shimmering robe.

"She is coming to the stream to bathe," said Liz, "when, in the distance, a roar is heard from the ice-capped mountains."

"Gawain," said Lucy, with a pang in her voice.

"Sitting on the highest peak," said Liz.

David pictured him surrounded by mist. He saw the hooked claws squeezing deep into the ice, boulder-sized pieces cracking away in the power of the mighty dragon's grip.

"He's amazing," said Lucy.

"Magnificent," said Liz. "The Lord of the Skies is a wonder of creation. And yet there is room in this noblest of hearts for the faintest glimmer of mortal sorrow. For he, Gawain, is the last of his kind: the very last dragon in the world."

"But he's not going to die. Not really," Lucy gabbled. "He's got to see Guinevere and . . ."

"Shush," went Liz, in a soothing voice. "Dream it gently. Watch as he spreads his spiky wings and glides in a spiral, down toward the caves."

"They're running!" cried Lucy. "The people are running!"

David saw people gathering children, herding them into the shelter of the caves.

"He has no wish to harm them," said Liz. "His thunderous roar is an echo for himself, a reminder of times gone by when many dragons filled these mountains. But yes, the people fear him. His blazing breath sets fire to the rocks. Trees bend to the song of his wings. He settles and his feet make craters in the earth."

"I dream it," said Lucy.

David gulped. He could almost feel the thud of the dragon's feet rattling every last rib in his chest.

"But Guinevere does not run away," said Liz. "She is there when Gawain bends down to drink. She looks boldly into his violet eyes. A wisp of smoke leaves the dragon's nose. He makes fire in the back of his throat. *Hrrr!*"

"*Hrrr!*" went Lucy.

"Ow," went David, banging his head against the wall as the force of the *hrring* made him jump.

"He's mad at her, because she isn't scared," said Lucy.

"A little," said Liz. "But curious, too. He decides he will test her courage. He threatens to burn her down to the tiniest cinder and blow her to the other side of the world. Guinevere shows no fear. She walks toward Gawain and asks him . . . what?"

"If she can sing to him!" Lucy exclaimed.

And suddenly the air was filled with song. Not a song with words or a hummable tune, but a gentle lullaby of growls and trills and warbles . . . and *hrrs*.

As the song washed over him, David began to feel strangely drowsy. The ice-capped mountains faded from his thoughts. The mighty Gawain put his head down . . . and slept.

But then, as quickly as the singing had begun, it ended with the sound of a gentle kiss. "Sleep tight, sweetheart. See you in the morning."

The floorboards creaked.

Liz. She was coming!

David shook himself awake and ducked into hiding. A second or two later, Liz appeared. She scuttled along the landing, Bonnington at her heels. "No, you go to David," she said, refusing Bonnington entry to the den.

David took a chance and raised his head, in time to see Liz reach out for the doorknob. For a moment, he thought about shouting a warning, but the words seemed to stick in the back of his throat. It was just as well they did.

Liz didn't jump. She didn't even wince.

She simply turned the knob once and disappeared inside, greeted by a very gentle *hrrr*.

SEEKING GAWAIN

What's going on?" David asked, pacing the kitchen, arms outstretched. "Come on, you've lived here longer than I have. Are those dragons real or what?"

Bonnington, sitting on a stool by the table, turned his head as the tenant swept by.

"And your human — what about her? Is she some sort of 'guardian' type? One of those 'special' people she was going on about? She's not normal, that's for sure. Any normal person would need hands like oven gloves to touch that doorknob. I could have been scarred for life."

Bonnington responded with a dragonlike yawn. As if by magic, a smell of burning filled the air. David dived toward the stove and yanked the grill pan away from the heat. Great. Two servings of badly charred toast. He glanced at his beans to check their progress. An orange volcano was forming in the pan. It erupted with a sort of alien *glop*, splattering its lava over the warmer. The tenant closed his eyes. Maybe it hadn't been such a good idea to make his own dinner, after all. But as several hours had now gone by since Liz had shut herself away in the den, it was either this or left-over gelatin or raid the cat's treats . . . or starve.

"Of course, she'll say it's a medical condition — like 'tennis elbow' or 'housekeeper's knee'." He grabbed a wooden spoon and stirred the beans that hadn't welded themselves to the bottom of the pan. " 'Potter's palm,' that's what she'll call it. She's always got some clever response."

Bonnington twizzled a sympathetic ear.

"It's all wrapped up with that story," said David, spreading his toast with lashings of butter, then glopping a hill of beans on top. "What did she mean 'the fire of Gawain is always in Lucy'? And how come he had violet eyes? She always paints them green. And what's this 'fire tear' thing? What's that all about? They don't cry sparks when they weep, do they? Is that why you shouldn't make them sniffly? They might set the house on fire?"

A-row, went Bonnington, choosing that moment to dab a paw at a rivulet of butter dripping from the toast in David's hands.

"Get off," said the tenant, jerking back and spraying beans across the tabletop. Terrific. He put down his toast and reached for a cloth. When he turned back, Bonnington was licking his plate.

David sighed. This wasn't his day. "All right," he conceded, "if you want it that badly you might as well have it." He whipped the plate from under Bonnington's nose and scraped the whole mess into the bowl marked CAT. Bonnington jumped down, sniffed at the beans — and promptly walked away.

"That's it," said David. "I'm going to bed."

Brr-rup, went Bonnington, and ran for the blanket.

◆   ◆   ◆

Sleep was a long time coming that night. No matter how tightly he cuddled Winston, played imaginary soccer, counted sheep, David just couldn't seem to drift off. To make matters worse, every time he closed his eyes, Liz's storytelling voice echoed through his mind.

Do you dream it, David?

The words beat like the throb of a drum.

Dream.

Like a song that wouldn't leave his head.

Dream.

Till the rhythm of it overpowered him, and his eyes became heavy and he did nod off.

Then, not surprisingly, a dream *did* come. A rather strange dream — about a dragon.

It began on the landing, outside the den. He was wearing his coat over his pajamas. He had a tea cozy on his head, a pair of oven gloves on his hands and a well-burned slice of toast in his pocket.

(But then, it *was* a dream.)

The door to the den was closed, the sign still warning him not to enter. This time he heeded it. Warily avoiding the polished handle, he knelt down and peeked through the keyhole instead.

A dragon's face peeked back.

It had huge, soppy, violet-colored eyes. But it wasn't made of clay. This dragon was *real*.

"Hello," David whispered dreamily to it.

The dragon blinked. Its scaly green ears pricked up and swiveled. David had a feeling he should know its name, but the dream wouldn't bring it to mind for the moment.

"Is Gawain in there?"

The dragon blew a wisp of smoke from its nose. It rolled its eyes and looked to one side. After a moment, it nodded its head.

"May I come in and see how he is?"

The dragon's mouth crinkled up at the edges. The eyes took on a worried expression. It slowly shook its head.

David patted his oven gloves together. "Are you a guard dragon?"

The dragon trilled proudly and paddled its feet. Another fine wisp of smoke hit the air.

"Come on, you can let me have a *little* peek," said David. "I'll give you this piece of toast if you do."

He took the bread from his pocket. The guard dragon's eyes lit up like sparklers. It looked quite interested in the idea of toast, especially the crispy blackened bits. David grinned. Rather strangely (even for a dream) he folded the toast into a tiny square and pushed it through the keyhole. It landed right at the guard dragon's feet. The dragon bent its head.

David raised one glove to the doorknob.

There was a rustle. The guard dragon stiffened its scales. It seemed to know it was being tricked.

In bed, David gave a nervous twitch. In his dream, he decided to risk the door.

"I only want to know what's going on," he whispered, and gripped the handle as he had before.

A blaze of fire left the guard dragon's mouth.

"YEOW!" cried David, and sat bolt upright.

Wide awake, flapping his hand.

In bed.

Bonnington, curled at the bottom of the blanket, burbled in annoyance and settled again.

"Sorry," David muttered. "Dragon dream, Bonners."

Bonnington gave a catty yawn. He lifted his head and fastened his copper-eyed gaze on the window.

David turned to look, anxiously wondering if a dragon wasn't there peering in through the glass. It was then he remembered that a dragon should have been peering *out* through the glass. Gadzooks. He wasn't on the windowsill.

David pulled on his bathrobe and puttered silently into the living room. Gadzooks was on the table where Lucy had left him. David lifted him into his hands. "You're a special dragon, aren't you?" he whispered. Gadzooks chewed the end of his pencil in silence. David ran a fingernail along the dragon's scales. A series of clinks echoed around the room. Yep, most definitely clay. "I must be going nuts," the tenant muttered. "Guard dragons. Special people. *Hrring* noises." He smiled and tapped Gadzooks's snout. "You're beautiful, but how can you possibly be real? Come on, your windowsill awaits."

And with that he carried Gadzooks to his room, completely unaware as he set him down of the tiny flash of light in the dragon's eye. A light that could have been anything at all: a reflection from the reading lamp on his desk, a flicker of moonlight over the Crescent or, if he'd truly believed in dragons, the gentle glimmer of a fire within.

DRAGON POX

The following morning, Liz had to come and shake David awake.

"Hey, sleepyhead, rise and shine. I've been tapping your door for the past ten minutes. Aren't you going to college today?"

David opened a bleary eye. He was lying on his bed in his bathrobe, Bonnington camped out on his chest.

"Wha'timeizzit?"

"Eight. Why aren't you in bed?"

"Couldn't sleep," the tenant muttered, pushing the cat aside. He sat up and shivered. "Dreamt about . . ." Well, perhaps he wouldn't say what he'd dreamt about.

Liz swept to the window and opened the curtains.

185

"Sorry if you felt ignored last night. I had to spend time with Lucy — and Gawain. I'll make you some breakfast when I finish loading the dishwasher." She picked a coffee-stained T-shirt off the floor, frowned and draped it over her arm. "Were you working late?" She tapped the computer. Multicolored fish were darting back and forth across the screen.

David yawned and ruffled his hair, showering Bonnington with early-morning dandruff. "I wrote another chapter of the *Snigger* story. Took ages. Like typing through molasses."

"Well, at least your fan club will be happy," said Liz, plucking a pair of boxer shorts off Winston's head. "When I went in to see Lucy this morning she was already deep into Chapter Six."

"*Mo-om?*"

A plaintive cry floated down the stairs.

"Talk of the little dragon." Liz marched across the room and yanked the door wide. "What?"

"Can I come down now, please?"

"No. Go back to bed."

A foot stamped hard against the landing.

"What's the matter?" asked David.

Liz sniffed at a crumpled sweater and immediately added that to her haul. "Struck down by the miseries: sore throat, prickly skin. Nothing to worry about. Common complaint in the Pennykettle household. She's just upset about breaking Gawain. She'll be fine in a couple of days."

David nodded. Should he ask about Gawain? Maybe. Maybe not. "I'll go up and see her after breakfast."

"Actually, I'd rather you didn't."

"It's OK," said David. "I've had every childhood illness there is. And she must be dying to know about Conker."

"She is, but I want her to rest. You can see her tonight, when you come home from college. So Conker's still with us?"

David tightened the belt of his bathrobe and

nodded. "He escaped with Snigger, in Henry's garden. I, um, reset the trap last night. You weren't around to ask . . . I hope you don't mind?"

Liz threw him a sideways look. A sock fell off the bundle of laundry. Bonnington sniffed at it and nearly keeled over. "Have you thought about what you're going to do if, by some chance, you manage to catch Conker?"

"Dunno. Take him to a vet, I s'pose."

"What about that envelope on the hall shelf? Couldn't those wildlife people help?"

David thought about the picture of Frankie the fox. Take Conker to a hospital? "Maybe," he shrugged.

"You could always talk to them when they call for the envelope."

"Um. Got to catch him first."

"Maybe they could give you some useful advice."

"The trap *works*," said David, sounding slightly irked. "We just have to lure Conker into it, that's all. I have Snigger on the case."

Liz raised an eyebrow.

"Where one squirrel goes, another follows — probably."

"You'd better go and look," said Liz.

David checked the trap immediately after breakfast. A snail had slithered over one of the acorns and the box was covered with fallen leaves, but there was no sign whatsoever of squirrel activity. To make matters worse, it was raining again.

Disappointed, he headed back to the house, whereupon the bathroom window opened. "David. Psst! Up here."

David halted on the patio and raised his eyes. "Lucy, go to bed. You're supposed to be ill."

"It's only dragon pox," she said, sounding hoarse. She stuck out her tongue and made a rasping *hrr-urrkkk!* "Didn't Mom tell you?"

"Not exactly," David muttered, blowing a raindrop off his nose. Dragon pox: another little Pennykettle joke, no doubt.

"What happened to Conker?"

"He ran away with Snigger. Look, I've got to —"

"Shush!" Lucy raised a hand for silence. "Phone! Come up and tell me, while Mom's gabbing."

"Lu-*cy*, I have to go to college. Besides, your mom said I wasn't allowed."

"She won't know," Lucy pleaded. "The man from Scrubbley Market calls today to tell Mom how many dragons he wants. They gab for ages. Please. I'm bored. Just five minutes."

David sighed and looked at his watch. "All right, five minutes."

"Great!" croaked Lucy, and banged the window shut.

She met him on the landing in her teddy bear pajamas and beckoned him eagerly into her room. "Come on, tell me what happened to Conker."

David plunked himself on the end of the bed and quickly related all the events in Mr. Bacon's garden. Lucy laughed out loud at the mower incident, but her face paled sharply at the mention of Caractacus.

"That crow?" she gasped. "That horrible crow?"

David nodded. "They're frightened of him. I think Caractacus might have attacked Conker once, and that's how his eye got hurt. It's just a wild guess, but I think a squirrel might have taken some eggs from his nest."

Lucy's gaze narrowed. "They wouldn't do *that*."

"They might, Luce, if they were desperate for food. No acorns, remember, when the oak tree was chopped down?"

"But Conker's a *nice* squirrel."

"I know," said David, in a comforting tone. "In the story, you never find out who raided the nest; Conker is just the unfortunate squirrel that Caractacus takes his revenge on." He reached into his coat and brought out several sheets of manuscript. "You can read it when I go to college. It's not true, remember, just . . . speculation."

Lucy took the papers and skimmed them excitedly. "You read it," she said, handing them back.

"Luce, I don't have time."

"Oh, *please*. Gruffen and Gwendolen want to hear."

David's gaze drifted to the far bedside table. In the space where Gawain normally sat, another dragon was perched beside Gwendolen. It was smaller than the female dragon and its wings were up as if poised to fly. With the curtains drawn and the table lamp on, Gruffen's features were lost in shadow, but David thought he remembered the name.

"Gruffen? Haven't I heard of him?"

"He normally sits by the door in the den."

Door, thought David, remembering keyholes and blazing fires. "He doesn't have violet eyes, does he?"

Lucy's gaze shifted sideways. "They're green," she whispered. "Read the story."

David glanced at his watch. Whatever happened now, he'd be late for his lecture. "All right. I'll read you the part where Conker tells Snigger what happened to his eye. This is just after they've escaped from the mower and they're sheltering themselves in their hiding place. This is what Conker says:

" 'I was on my way home to my drey in the roof when Caractacus saw me coming. He was on me before I knew it, pecking at my head with his thick, blunt beak. He was flapping his wings and cawing like crazy, screaming that I was a thief and a killer. He dug his sharp claws into my back. I twisted and bit his foot. I got one of his toes, I think.'

'Toes?' said Snigger.

'I bit it off,' gulped Conker."

"Ugh!" said Lucy.

David turned a page. " 'After I bit him, he squawked and flew away. I scrambled down the branch as fast as I could, but my eye was blurry and I couldn't see where I was going. I heard Caractacus coming again. He swooped and I lost my balance. I fell through lots of leaves and branches and the next thing I knew, everything went dark. When I woke up I was on the ground. I couldn't see anything out of my bad eye. I tried to climb the sycamore tree, but I got dizzy and kept falling. I knew then that I'd never see my drey again.' "

"That's terrible!" Lucy shouted. "I hate that Caractacus!"

"Calm down," said David, holding her wrist. "It's just a story. You'll make your throat sore."

"It's *not* just a story!" Lucy insisted. "Where's he hiding?"

"Hiding?" said David, releasing his grip. He flexed his fingers. His hands felt . . . prickly.

"You said Conker had a hiding place! Where?"

David rubbed his brow. Now *that* felt prickly. "Um, they're hiding in a watering can in a pile of junk near Mr. Bacon's shed."

"Go and look," said Lucy. "You've got to look, *now*."

But David was busy looking at his hands. "What's this?" he said, jumping to his feet. His skin looked *scaly* and . . . *green*. "Oh no!" he squeaked. "I've got dragon pox!"

WRITER'S BLOCK

Well, that'll teach you not to go where you shouldn't," said a voice.

Liz, arms folded, appeared in the doorway.

"Oops," went Lucy, sliding under the blanket.

"I thought I told you she was resting, David?"

"I know. I'm sorry. I was only . . . Liz, help. My skin is all *scaly*." He held out his hands for Liz to inspect.

She flicked them a cursory glance.

"Let me look," said Lucy, sitting up.

"You stay there," Liz scolded. "I'll have a word with you in a moment. I'm sure David didn't get up here by chance."

Lucy shrank back, protesting loudly.

"Shouldn't we call the doctor?" David gulped.

"A doctor couldn't do much for that."

David blinked in panic. "You mean . . . normal people can't be cured? I'm going to turn into a dragon?"

"What's he going on about?" said Lucy, wrinkling her nose.

"This," sighed Liz. She licked a finger and pressed it into David's palm. The "scales" lifted off with ease. She switched on the room light and showed him the result.

"That's glitter," said Lucy, checking her arms. "And *he* thought it was dragon scales!" She threw back her head and cackled with laughter.

"Time that someone went to college," said Liz.

David's worry lines morphed into a scowl.

"No, he has to look for Conker!" coughed Lucy, just as a thunderclap rattled the windows.

"Well, he'd better wear a good pair of boots," said Liz.

David frowned and parted the curtains.

Rain was bouncing off the rooftops.

◆ ◆ ◆

It hammered on the trash cans and overflowed the gutters. It pelted the windows and swamped the drains. David watched it from the kitchen window. There was no going to college in a downpour like this. And certainly no hope of searching for Conker. He clomped off to his room and shut himself inside.

It was lunchtime before he emerged. Liz was in the kitchen, preparing a salad. The tenant tramped in and yanked the fridge open. He swigged a drink from a carton of juice, banged it back and slammed the fridge shut.

"Is it me," said Liz, shaking drops of water from some lettuce, "or do I sense an *atmosphere* around you today?"

"It's this weather," David grumbled, sinking into a chair. "Can't get anything done."

Liz glanced through the window. The rain was still teeming. "The weather doesn't stop you from doing homework, does it?"

"I did my work," David said glumly. "It's all about weather fronts, anyway."

"Well, write some more of your story, then. That usually makes you happy."

"Been trying to. Nothing will come. It was like this last night, but not as bad. I think I've got writer's block."

"Lovely," Liz muttered, grating a carrot. "One with dragon pox; the other with writer's block."

"But it was going so *well* last week. I can't understand what I'm doing wrong. I'm right at the exciting part where Snigger is going to get Conker to the nutbox, but whenever I start, I just get . . . stuck. I can't get a single good idea."

Liz blew a wayward curl off her brow. "Isn't Gadzooks any help?"

"Pff!" went David. "He deserted me."

"Don't be silly. A special dragon wouldn't do that."

"Well, how else do you explain his pencil breaking?"

Liz gave him a quizzical look.

"Last night, when I was stuck with my chapter, I

closed my eyes and imagined him writing — and he ground his pencil till the tip snapped off! I tried again just now and he threw down his pad and disappeared in a puff of green smoke!"

"Oh dear," Liz sighed, "that's really unruly. What have you done to upset him?"

"Nothing," said David, as if the suggestion was ludicrous anyway.

Liz frowned and shook her head. "Well, we can't have dragons having tantrums. Something needs to be done about that."

"I banished him to the bookcase," David muttered.

Down the hall, the doorbell rang.

Liz reached for a towel and wiped her hands. "Well, that's not right, punishing him. He loves that window. He won't like being stuck in a dark corner."

"Liz, he's made of clay," David sighed. "He doesn't know the difference between a bookcase and a windowsill."

Elizabeth Pennykettle bristled noticeably. "Well, if

that's what you think of him, no wonder he won't help you." She took off her apron and went to the door.

David buried his face in his hands. I'm living in a madhouse, he told himself. I'm living with people who get dragon pox and think clay things enjoy a garden view. What am I *doing* here?

"Oh yes," said Liz, down the hall. "Step in for a minute, you must be soaked."

"Thank you," a female voice replied.

David slid his hands away from his eyes. He leaned back in his chair and peered down the hall. A young woman, about his own age, was wiping her feet on the coconut-fiber mat. Her caramel-colored, thigh-length jacket was damp with several patches of rain. Her dark green tights looked uncomfortably clammy. The small umbrella she was fighting to close was dripping water all over the carpet. She sneezed and the sudden jerk of her head made her look up and catch sight of David. She blushed and offered him a little smile. David forced himself to grimace back.

"What a time to be collecting these," Liz said, opening the envelope from the Wildlife Hospital. She rifled through her purse. "David, have you got any change?"

David rose from his seat and ambled down the hall. The visitor shifted her weight to one hip, angling one knee across the other. David glanced at her ID badge, held to her coat with a safety pin. *Sophie Prentice, wildlife volunteer.* He raised his eyes and had a good look at her. She was tall and slim with copper-blonde hair that framed her plain, but attractive face. Her eyes had a gentle, inquisitive look, as if everything she saw were slightly unfocused. She coughed uncertainly and flicked her head. A raindrop glistened on her strong, dark eyebrows.

David delved into his pocket for coins.

"Well done," said Liz, and tipped his hand so that every last coin poured into the envelope.

"Liz-zz? That's all I've —"

"He's very giving," Liz said, sealing the flap.

"Especially when he's in a good mood." She handed Sophie the envelope.

"Thank you, that's very generous," Sophie said shyly, dropping it into a plastic bag.

David sighed in defeat and pushed his hands into his pockets.

"It sounds like a very good cause," said Liz.

"It is," said Sophie, glad to have the chance to justify David's grand donation. "We take care of lots of sick animals at the hospital. Badgers, birds —"

"Squirrels?" said a husky voice. "Do you take care of them?"

Lucy was sitting in the middle of the stairs.

"Yes," said Sophie, smiling at her. "Any kind of wildlife."

"There's an injured squirrel in our garden," said Liz.

Sophie's gray eyes flickered with interest.

Lucy clomped downstairs to stand by her mom. "His name is Conker and he can't see well. We're going to catch him and take him to the library gardens."

"Oh?" went David. This was news to him.

Sophie thought carefully for a moment then said, "If he has a bad eye, you could bring him to us. Our vet will check him over, absolutely free. Shall I give you one of our leaflets?"

Lucy gave an uncertain shrug.

Sophie felt in her pocket and pulled out a folded leaflet and a pen. "Our telephone number's on here. I'll give you my cell number, too — in case you need me after hours." She scribbled down the number and held the leaflet out.

Lucy's hand went up to take it. Liz intercepted and handed it to David. "Thank you, that's very helpful."

Sophie nodded bashfully and edged toward the door. Outside the rain beat gently on the path. "Well, nice to meet you. Don't hesitate to call. Thanks again for the donation." She glanced at David. His gaze dropped to the leaflet. "Bye," Sophie whispered, and turned up her collar.

Liz had all but closed the door when David blurted, "Are they intelligent? Squirrels, I mean?"

Sophie paused on the step. "Hmm," she said, with

a gentle nod. "They're very resourceful, good at over-coming obstacles and such."

"You don't think we're wasting our time — trying to catch it?"

Sophie tilted her head. A dolphin-shaped earring scraped the collar of her coat. "No," she said in a voice that was little more than a murmur. "You're doing it because you care about him, aren't you?"

There was silence then. Lucy bit her lip.

"Call if you need me," Sophie said again, and this time, with a click of her umbrella, she was gone.

"I like her," said Lucy as Liz closed the door.

"Yes," said Liz. "She's very unassuming. Lovely smile too. Didn't you think so, David?"

"She's got interesting eyebrows," he said.

"He likes her," sniffed Lucy. "Can I look at the leaflet?"

Liz guided her back to the stairs. "No. Let David study it first. Now that he's met someone from the Wildlife Hospital, I'm sure he'll want to ask for advice on all sorts of things. Now come on, madam, back to bed. You're supposed to be resting, remember?"

Lucy pouted and stomped up the stairs.

As David turned to go, Liz tapped him on the shoulder. "Make up with him, David."

"Who?"

"Your dragon, that's who. If you want his spark to stay lit, you have to love him — remember?"

David pulled a face and dragged off to his room.

He went straight to the bookcase and crouched beside Gadzooks. "All right, I'm sorry. I love you, *really*." He *hrred* on the dragon's snout and polished it. "There. You don't get that every day. Come on, vacation's over." And he reached out and picked Gadzooks up off the shelf and returned him safely to the windowsill.

To look out over the garden once more.

DO NOT 'DISTRUB'

The following day, the rain had slowed to a tolerable drizzle and David did get away to college — not that he really got much done. He played foosball with a couple of friends, collected an essay from the departmental office and attended a lecture on global cooling in something called the Pleistocene Age. It could have been snowballing in the Plasticine Age. His mind wasn't much on geography at all.

It was lost in *Snigger and the Nutbeast*.

In total contrast to the previous day, his mind had been buzzing with ideas all morning. So much so that by midafternoon he skipped the Camera Club meeting and practically sprinted home from college.

Throwing his coat on a hook, he dived into his

room, started his computer and quickly reopened the *Snigger* file. *Chapter Eight*, he typed. *Conker found*. Yes, this was it. He could feel the creative excitement building, sense the ideas flowing again. He could feel — *dunk*, the weight of a tabby cat landing in his lap.

"Not now, Bonners." With an effortless swing he lobbed the cat, underarm, onto the bed. "No interruptions," David warned him, just as he heard Liz shout.

"Lucy, can you come into the kitchen, please?"

Lucy? Up and about again? She really MUST be avoided. Grabbing an orange felt-tipped pen, he scribbled out a message on a large scrap of paper and taped it surreptitiously to the outside of his door.

Shortly afterward, Lucy clomped downstairs. Her footsteps halted outside his room. "Mom," David heard her say, "what does 'DO NOT DISTRUB' mean?"

More footsteps announced Liz's presence in the hall. "It looks to me like a note written in haste by a person who would not appreciate another person bursting into his room right now — even if she knocked extremely politely."

"But the rain stopped. That means the person can go squirrel hunting."

"No," said Liz, her voice growing fainter as she moved toward the kitchen. "It means that one particular person is going to help her mother hang out some laundry."

"Oh, but my dragon pox is really bad now."

"Lucy, don't lie. Get the clothespins."

Lucy's voice trailed off with a glum-sounding, "Ohh . . ."

David clenched his fists in triumph and swung his chair around to face the computer.

Within minutes he had typed his opening paragraph:

At last, the rain had stopped hammering on the watering can. Snigger woke with a start and crept toward the light. He poked his whiskers out of the hole. The world dripped with the scent of warm, moist air. Sparrows twittered. Trees rustled in the breeze. An eager spider was spinning its web between the handle of the can and the spout itself. Snigger took a deep and nervous breath. He knew that the time had come. The time to make the dangerous journey to the nutbox. He reversed his body back into the can and gently nudged Conker awake.

"We're in business," David said to Gadzooks.

Gadzooks stared silently into the garden, where Liz and Lucy were hanging out the laundry.

David's fingers flew across the keyboard. With every sentence, every word, the two squirrels moved closer to the Pennykettles' garden . . .

Snigger led the way to the garden fence. He quickly found the panel with the hole at the bottom and anxiously waited for Conker to catch up. The one-eyed squirrel was limping badly. His thin gray body, weak with hunger, was barely able to drag along the ground. As he reached Snigger's side he almost collapsed.

"Leave me," he whispered. "Please. Get away. You're in danger, too, if Caractacus comes."

At the mention of that name every hair on Snigger's

body bristled with fear. But from somewhere deep within he found the courage to say, "No, we're going together," and he nudged Conker headfirst through the hole.

"Get the support, please."

David paused and glanced into the garden. Liz was hanging out a red wool sweater. The line was almost filled with laundry. He watched Lucy bring the clothes support over and saw the clothes hoisted like a row of flags. Wondering what a squirrel would make of that, he turned his fingers to the keyboard again . . .

"What's that?" said Snigger, following Conker through the hole.

Conker looked up with his one good eye. A line of clothes was flapping in the breeze. "Don't know," he shrugged. "My mother said that my father could run along that wire. She said he escaped from Bonnington once by going up that wooden thing, there, in the middle. Bonnington followed, but he fell right off."

Snigger flagged an eager tail. He wouldn't mind

having a turn on that wire. But games could wait until Conker was safe. He squinted at the sycamore tree, trying to pick out the shape of a crow. The sycamore's branches struggled in the wind. Caractacus wasn't among them.

"Which way?" Conker asked.

Snigger turned his attention to the pile of rocks on the far side of the garden. Behind those rocks lay food and shelter. One good run and Conker would be safe. All they had to do was cross the lawn . . .

"Hmm," muttered David, sitting back, frowning. He drummed his fingers on the mouse pad a moment. Crossing the lawn would be dangerous in daylight. A sharp-eyed crow would spot them with ease. They'd go around the borders, wouldn't they? Take cover among the leafier plants? Then again, Liz's garden was long and narrow. So maybe a quick dash would be better? Despite the risk of sudden attack? Undecided, he consulted Gadzooks.

The dragon seemed to have sharpened his pencil. In

a flash David pictured him scribbling something. Something unexpected:

Bonnington

David glanced over his shoulder at the cat.

Bonnington was staring rigidly at the window. His ears were pricked, his copper eyes wide on full alert.

"What's the matter?" David said, reaching out to stroke him.

Bonnington snaked away. He leapt off the bed, scuttled to the door and immediately started to paw the frame.

David frowned. This was very odd. Why would Gadzooks write Bonnington's name when Bonnington had nothing to do with the story? He started to type again.

"*I think we should go across the lawn,*" said Snigger.

Conker's whiskers started to twitch. He studied the long expanse of grass.

"*We'll run to the bird feeder first,*" Snigger added. "*And hide in the shadows until you're ready.*"

A-row-row-oo! Bonnington yowled. His claws screeched against the painted door. David winced but continued typing.

Snigger hopped onto the edge of the lawn. The sky was a swimming, cloudy blue. He checked the chimney holes, the treetops, the gutters, the fence posts. All the places where a bird might perch. He couldn't see Caractacus anywhere. Warily, he started to make his move . . .

From somewhere in the garden Lucy shouted: "Mom! Quick! Look over there!"

"Oh yes," said Liz. "Well, I never . . ."

David paused and glanced through the window. Lucy and her mom were out of sight — somewhere near the kitchen, by the sound of it. Unable to see what it was that they'd spotted, he shrugged and went back to the story again.

Snigger turned back toward the flower bed.

"Oh no, he's going," Lucy said faintly.

"If he comes," said Snigger. "I'll lead him away."

"No!" cried Conker. "He'll get you for sure!"

Snigger glanced at the clothesline. "I'll run along the wire."

"No!" *chattered Conker, panting with fright.*

"He'll follow me first — then you can escape. Just look for the rocks — and the acorns in the grass. You can scent your way from there."

"It's too dangerous," Conker protested.

But Snigger was already on the move, heading for the bird feeder in the middle of the lawn . . .

In the garden, Lucy clapped her hands. "Look, Mom! See! I told you! I told you!"

"Run and get David," David heard Liz say.

"Oh, please, not now," he groaned. "Not when I'm at the crucial —"

Agggghhhhhhhh!

A scream rang out like a fire alarm.

David was on his feet so fast his chair toppled over and hit the floor. He turned to the window. Liz's face filled the pane. "Quickly!" she beckoned, rapping the glass.

David whipped around. By the door, Bonnington was hissing and spitting as if a large gang of tomcats had invaded the room. Suddenly, Lucy burst in, gasping so much she could hardly speak.

Bonnington shot past her, into the hall.

"What's going on?" David asked.

"He's here," Lucy panted, heaving at the effort.

"Who's here?"

"*Caractacus!*"

David's shoulders turned to ice.

"He saw Snigger on the lawn! He's trying to get him!"

David's mouth tried to spill the words. "But that's impossible. I'm just writing that . . ."

"*Come on!*" Lucy screamed. "He's going to kill him!"

She shook her fists and ran.

For a moment, David was too stunned to move. He stared at the computer, then at Gadzooks.

"You knew," he said. "You were trying to warn me."

And he turned and hurtled after Lucy.

CONKER FOUND

"Oh, thank goodness!" Liz exclaimed, as David skidded to a halt beside her. She pointed urgently up the garden. Caractacus was perched on the roof of the bird feeder. He was stepping sideways along the ridge, his head making downward jerking movements, his sharp eyes scanning the lawn for movement.

"Where's Snigger?"

"We're not really sure," said Liz. "We saw two squirrels near the garden fence and watched them hop out onto the lawn. Lucy was running to get you when the crow swooped down — off the shed, I think. In the panic, I didn't see what happened next. The squirrels might have fled."

"No, Snigger's there!" Lucy shouted.

David followed her pointing finger, in time to see Snigger hop out from the fins that formed the feet of the bird feeder. Caractacus spotted the movement right away. His wings went out like big black parachutes. Snigger made a nervous, darting run — then stopped, perilously, to peek over his shoulder. Caractacus dropped with devastating speed. "No!" squealed Lucy as Snigger made a terrified chattering noise and narrowly escaped the lunging claws. He dashed back to the safety of the feeder legs. Caractacus rasped and spat in anger. One swift beat of his powerful wings took him back to the bird feeder roof.

"Go away!" screamed Lucy, charging forward.

Caractacus turned and screeched at her.

"Lucy, get back here!" David cried. He snaked an arm around her waist and scooped her up, kicking and punching, off the ground.

"Let me go!" she railed. "I have to save Conker."

"If Caractacus attacks you, you're going to get hurt."

"Lucy, you stay right here!" Liz ordered, gathering

217

her up and clamping her tight. In the same breath she shouted: "David, look!"

To David's horror, while Caractacus had been distracted by Lucy, Snigger had made another dash from the feeder. This time he was well into the middle of the lawn, chattering and flagging his bushy gray tail as if he were inviting the crow to come.

Caractacus took to the air once more.

Snigger twitched in fright — and ran.

Not to the bird feeder. Not to the rock garden.

"I don't believe it," said David. "He's going for the clothesline!"

"My laundry!" Liz exclaimed as Snigger scuttled up the angled clothes support.

"What's he *doing*?" Lucy fretted, shaking her fists. "Caractacus will easily get him there."

He's drawing him away, thought David. Just like the story. He wants Caractacus to follow so Conker can escape. *He's trying to save Conker's life.*

"Watch the bird feeder!" David shouted to Lucy. "See if Conker runs to the rock garden."

"What are *you* going to do?" Liz asked, looking worried.

"Cover Snigger's back," the tenant said, rapidly uncoiling the garden hose.

By now, Snigger was on the line, scrambling and tumbling over the clothespins. Caractacus banked and came swooping in again. But as David took aim with the nozzle of the hose, another character entered the scene.

Bonnington shot out from under the bench. With a spiraling leap the cat stretched upward and clawed at the crow's soft underbelly. Caractacus screeched in fear. A cluster of his feathers fluttered to earth. He beat his wings and tried to change course. Too late. With a squawk, he plowed into Liz's bright red sweater, claws catching and tangling in the loose woolen threads. Bonnington turned and leapt again, this time taking a tail feather.

David immediately switched his aim. Although Caractacus was technically the villain of the piece, David had no desire to see him dead. "Sorry, kitty," he muttered and fired at Bonnington.

Click. No water left the spout.

Idiot! He'd forgotten to turn on the faucet!

He hurled the hose aside — and ran.

By now, Caractacus was back in the air, but was stuck on the line by Liz's sweater. No matter how hard the big bird flapped, his claws would not break free of the threads. Suddenly, he crashed to a vertical position, one foot swinging free of the wool. And there he dangled, on one snagged leg, tired and helpless and at Bonnington's mercy.

The cat prepared to spring.

"No!" yelled David.

With one decisive lunge he grabbed Bonnington by the scruff of the neck and yanked him clear. "Good guard cat. Time for some cat treats." The cat hissed and bared his teeth. David beckoned Liz and Lucy forward.

"Is he dead?" hissed Lucy, glancing at the crow as David handed Bonnington to Liz.

"No," said David, "he's frightened and in pain. I'll need your help to free him."

"But he tried to kill Snigger."

"I suppose he was defending his territory," said Liz. "He's going to break a wing if you don't untangle him."

"Right," said David, cupping his hands around Caractacus's body and lifting the bird to take the weight off his foot. He twisted his hands to keep the dagger-like bill away from Lucy's fingers. "Come on, he won't hurt you."

Lucy stepped forward, biting her lip. Bravely, she gripped one wrinkly toe. Caractacus let out a high-pitched *caw* and flicked his wedge-shaped tail in protest. Lucy squealed but didn't let go. She slipped the wool off the claw with ease.

As she moved to the next toe, she stopped again. "That's where Conker bit him, look." She tilted the foot for David to see. Caractacus had a shortened toe.

"Oh yes," said David. "Gosh, how strange. I must have noticed it subconsciously when I saw him on the fence post."

"What does subconsciously mean?"

"Oh, you might just say Gadzooks told me."

Lucy looked puzzled. "I thought he did."

Before David could comment, Liz called out: "How are you doing? I can't hold Bonny much longer."

"Finished," said David, righting Caractacus as Lucy unraveled the last few threads.

The crow's dark eyes darted hopefully at the sky. "Be good," David whispered and opened his hands. Caractacus flapped off with a moody *squawk*.

David immediately looked up the garden. "Did anyone see where Snigger went?"

"He wriggled down the leg of your jeans," said Lucy.

"He did *what*?" said Liz, spilling Bonnington from her arms.

Everyone turned and looked at the laundry.

The right leg of David's jeans looked *unusually lumpy*, just below the knee.

"He's stuck," said Lucy.

"Well, he'd better get unstuck," Liz said dourly. "If he messes in those jeans, there's going to be trouble."

"Let's get him in the hutch," said David. He hurried to the rock garden, grabbed the nutbox and laid it on its back near the clothesline. While Liz removed the clothespins, he clamped his hands tight around the leg of the jeans above and below the bump at the knee. "Get ready," he said, lowering the jeans into the body of the box and giving them a gentle shake. An indignant chattering filled the air. Then *whoosh!* The bump in the jeans disappeared and a squirrel shot into the hutch.

Lucy slammed the door shut. "Got him!" she clapped.

"Good," said David with a whistle of relief. "One down. One to go. Now, where's Conker?"

A-ROW-WOW-OO! a familiar voice cried.

Everyone turned together.

Bonnington was standing in the middle of the lawn.

He was holding a squirrel between his teeth.

THE WILDLIFE
HOSPITAL

Before anyone could move or say another word, Bonnington padded across the lawn and dropped his catch at David's feet.

Meow, he went, looking pleased with himself.

Liz put a hand across her mouth. "Please don't tell me he killed it."

Lucy threw herself into her mother's arms and couldn't bear to look.

David crouched down and stroked Bonnington's head. Even if the cat had made a kill, he couldn't be blamed for doing what came naturally to him: hunting and bringing his spoils back home.

"Is it Conker?" Liz asked.

David looked down at the limp gray body. The

squirrel was lying curled on its side. The eye in view was tightly closed. It didn't look particularly damaged or matted.

"I need to turn him over," David said, and put a careful hand around the animal's stomach.

The squirrel immediately started to quiver. Its toes curled inward and its body twitched in violent spasms as if it were having some kind of fit. Uncertain of what to do for it, David rested a hand on its body and prayed the little creature wouldn't die of fright. Thankfully, after about fifteen seconds, the convulsions eased and it lay back, panting.

David closed a hand around it again and gently lifted it off the ground. "Can someone open the trap?"

Lucy knelt by the box. Keeping a watchful eye on Snigger, she carefully slid the door half open. As David eased himself toward it, the stricken squirrel raised its head. There was a crusted wound above its closed right eye.

"It's him," Lucy whispered.

David nodded. "He's not doing well, Luce."

"Yes," she sniffed, touching Conker's tail.

David glanced up at Liz.

"You'd better give Sophie a call," she said.

The Wildlife Hospital was set on a farm about five miles north of the Scrubbley town center. Just beyond a small field dotted with sheep, Liz turned onto a narrow dirt track that quickly opened out into a cobbled courtyard, flanked by a number of redbrick buildings. A goat looked up from a wooden trough. Two ducks waddled away from the car. A long-haired cat, sunbathing in a wheelbarrow, lifted its smoke-gray head and yawned. On a wall of the old stone farmhouse was a hand-painted sign: LIDDIKER'S ORGANIC PRODUCE. A list of vegetables and their prices per pound were chalked up on a board beside it. Next to that was a sign for a riding school. Just above it, a silhouetted picture of a fox with a bandage around its paw. The words SCRUBBLEY WILDLIFE HOSPITAL framed the fox's head.

"Is this it?" said Lucy, unimpressed.

"Hmm," went Liz, parking the car alongside a rusted

water pump. "Might buy some potatoes while we're here."

"There's Sophie," said David, pointing ahead to a moss-covered archway.

Sophie was walking slowly toward them, leading a large black horse. She was wearing a pair of tight brown pants, faintly splattered with grass and mud. A loose green shirt hung around her shoulders. Her collar was up, her hair pinned back with a butterfly clip. Her cheeks were glowing gently as if she'd recently returned from riding.

Lucy hurried over, arms wide open. "You've got a horse," she said.

"This is Major," said Sophie, tugging the reins as Major snorted and tossed his head. "He's my very best friend in the world." She brought Major's head down over her shoulder so Lucy could stroke his dark, sleek nose.

"Can I ride him?"

"He's too big for you," said Liz.

"We have ponies." Sophie's gray eyes flashed.

"Ponies?"

"I think not," said Liz. She put a motherly hand under Lucy's chin and gently pushed her mouth shut.

Sophie smiled and changed the subject. "You found your injured squirrel, then?"

David lifted the hutch from the car. "He's in a bad way."

Sophie gave a concerned little nod. "They usually are if they turn up here. Give me a moment and I'll take you in. Mrs. Wenham, the lady who runs the hospital, is expecting you."

With a click of her tongue, Sophie led Major across the yard to a stable smelling of warm, clean hay. She exchanged brief words with another girl, patted Major's shoulder and stepped out into the sunlight again.

"This way," she smiled, skipping two sunken concrete steps and entering a room at the back of the house. It had the clinical smell of a veterinary practice but looked like a slightly understocked pet shop. There were cans of food in trays by the window, bags of seed and pellets and grain, a large stack of buckets, several piles of blankets, and shelves full of medicines, rubber gloves and tissues. Against the far wall was a stack of cages. David spotted a hedgehog in one and a jay with a splinted wing in another. He was wondering if this would be Conker's fate — a cage, in this room — when Sophie announced, "Here's Mrs. Wenham."

A portly lady with wavy black hair and a chubby red face came in to join them. "Now then, what do we have here?" Her question was addressed primarily to Lucy. "Injured squirrel, if I'm not mistaken?"

"His name is Conker," said Lucy. "He's got a bad eye."

"Oh dear," said Mrs. Wenham. "We'd better take a look."

David laid the hutch on a long, metal table and turned it around for Mrs. Wenham to see.

"Poor thing," she said, with a wheezy stoop. "How did he get like that?"

"A crow got him," Lucy replied.

"We think that's what happened," David explained.

Mrs. Wenham clicked her tongue. "Goodness, he's thinner than a piece of string. Just a youngster, too. Look at that tail. I've seen tinsel in better shape than that. How long has he been like this?"

"Ages," said Lucy. "Since before David came."

"She means a few months," said Liz.

Mrs. Wenham nodded. "Well, you were right to bring him to us. He's certainly not a healthy squirrel. Any other problems, apart from his eye?"

"Mr. Bacon doesn't like him," Lucy said.

Sophie chuckled behind her hand.

"He had a shaking fit," David said, sparing Mrs. Wenham any further confusion.

Mrs. Wenham frowned as she took this in. She bent down and tapped the mesh. "Come on, sweetie. Look this way."

Conker, who seemed to have regained some strength, sat up and flagged his stringy tail.

"That wound's been infected," Mrs. Wenham said. "Mr. Deans will want to see that."

"He's the vet," said Sophie. "He'll be coming in

tomorrow. He's wonderful. He charges next to nothing to treat our animals."

"We'll pay for whatever Conker needs," said Liz.

Sophie shook her head. "It's all done through donations. In a sense, you've already paid. Well, David has." She flicked a bashful smile his way.

"Hang on," Mrs. Wenham interrupted, angling her square-shaped head, "is it me, or are there two squirrels in this box?"

"That's Snigger," said Lucy. "He followed David home from the library gardens when David stole some acorns for the trap."

David grimaced and looked out the window.

"And what's wrong with Snigger?"

"Nothing," said Liz, "as far as we know."

"He's Conker's friend," Lucy piped up. "He saved Conker from the mower in Mr. Bacon's garden and ran up the clothesline when Caractacus came."

Mrs. Wenham lifted an eyebrow.

"You can read it in David's story."

"You write stories?" asked Sophie.

"A one-time thing," David said, blushing.

"He'll do one for your birthday if you ask him," said Lucy.

"Lucy, enough," said Liz. "What happens now, Mrs. Wenham? Will you be able to take them in?"

Mrs. Wenham puffed her cheeks. "The injured one, yes. But Snigger — well, he's a different matter. We're not allowed to keep healthy animals here."

"But you have to!" Lucy protested fiercely. "Conker will miss him if Snigger goes away."

That started a general debate, with Liz, David *and* Mrs. Wenham all chattering away at once. Sophie eventually broke it up.

"Couldn't . . . ?" she said, holding onto the word so long that David almost wanted to pinch her. "Couldn't they stay together for company, Mrs. Wenham? They don't seem to mind being cooped up in a hutch, so the aviary pen won't present a problem."

"Aviary?" said Liz.

"Through here," said Sophie. She nudged David's foot and nodded at the rabbit hutch.

David, quick to see what she was planning, grabbed the hutch and followed her outside. Right away they came upon a wire-screened cage containing nothing but a couple of metal dishes, a few bird boxes and several enormous sawn-off branches.

Sophie unlatched the aviary door and beckoned David swiftly inside. "Let them go," she hissed, "before Mrs. W. kicks up a fuss."

"Sophie?" Mrs. Wenham called. "You know we're not allowed —"

"This is perfect for woodland animals," piped Sophie. "These branches came from an oak, so the squirrels will feel at home in here."

"Sophie, it's against —"

"Look," said Lucy, arriving quickly. She beckoned Mrs. Wenham to the aviary door.

Conker was out of the hutch already, nibbling at the tip of a sunflower seed.

"He likes it," Lucy said.

Mrs. Wenham smiled graciously. "Yes, my love, he's welcome to stay, but —"

"There's Snigger!"

David turned to see where Lucy was pointing. Snigger had scrambled to the top of the branches and was busily inspecting the entrance to a bird box. He darted out of sight as Mrs. Wenham stepped toward him.

Liz arrived in the aviary then, and while Lucy continued to argue her point with both her mom *and* Mrs. Wenham, David moved closer to Sophie and whispered, "Thanks — you know — for helping them."

Sophie folded her arms and nodded. A strand of hair worked loose from her clip and fell across her cheek like a piece of straw. "It's OK," she said quietly. "That's what I'm here for. I've always liked animals . . . and people who care for them."

David threw her a sideways glance. Sophie pressed her lips together as if she was slowly sucking a candy. A pinkish tinge spread across her cheeks.

David rearranged some stones with his toe. "Um, I don't suppose you'd like to —?"

"He can stay!" cried Lucy, barging between them.

"Mrs. Wenham says it's all right!" She sprang up on her toes in front of Sophie.

David looked at the sky, muttering something under his breath.

"It's highly irregular," Mrs. Wenham said, "but as Snigger seems to be your leading character, we'd better not let him go just yet."

"When will Conker be better?" pressed Lucy.

Sophie smiled and swung her hands. "We'll let Mr. Deans look at Conker tomorrow, then we'll give you a call."

Lucy nodded and leaned in close. "You will take really good care of him, won't you?"

"My personal project," Sophie assured her.

"Watch Snigger, he's a handful," muttered David.

Chuk! went Snigger, back at the bird box.

"I can handle him," Sophie laughed. She rubbed Lucy's arm. "They'll be fine with us. I'll call you when I've got some news. I promise."

OH, SOPHIE

It was Saturday afternoon before Sophie called, four long days since the journey to the hospital. David was sprawled out on his bed, editing a chapter of *Snigger and the Nutbeast,* when the telephone rang in the living room.

"Just a moment. I'll call him," he heard Liz answer. "Da-vid! Sophie for you!"

David practically fell off the bed. He snatched up a comb, tidied his hair, realized how utterly pointless that was and headed for the phone — only to find that Lucy had beaten him to it.

"It's me, Lucy! Is Conker all right?"

"Thank *you*," Liz yanked the phone from her grasp. "Sorry," she apologized to Sophie. "There seems to be some strange interference on the line. Here's David now."

Lucy stamped her foot.

Liz bustled her into the hall. "Out. Sophie wants to talk to David in private."

"Why can't *I* talk to her?"

"Because you're not a handsome young man."

"Well, neither is he!"

"Kitchen," said Liz.

And that was that.

As it happened, David was off the phone in less than two shakes of a squirrel's tail.

"That was quick," said Liz, as he joined them at the table. "What's the news on Conker?"

"I'm not sure," said David, looking perplexed. "Sophie didn't want to say on the phone. She's coming by in twenty minutes."

"Goodness," said Liz. "Plates, Lucy."

"Huh," went Lucy in a toady voice. "David's *girlfriend* is coming to lunch."

◆　◆　◆

There was fruit cake and an egg custard and a lemon meringue pie, and pyramids of tuna and cucumber sandwiches. When David saw the size of the spread he made a mental note to invite Sophie over as often as he could. Sophie herself seemed quite astonished that Liz had gone to so much trouble.

"Nonsense," said Liz. "Come on, dig in. David, why don't you get Sophie a drink?"

David moved to the counter. "What would you like?"

"Something herbal would be nice."

"Top cabinet," said Liz. "There's a range of flavors."

David found them. He chose a rosehip tea bag and dropped it in a mug.

"Is Conker all right now?" Lucy chipped in. It was the third time she'd asked since Sophie had arrived.

Sophie sat forward and pushed a grain of salt across the table. "I'm afraid I've got good news and bad news about Conker."

"Oh dear," said Liz, feeding Bonnington some tuna.

David winced. The electric kettle clicked off.

"Bad news?" Lucy's bottom lip started to quiver.

Sophie reached over and touched her hand. "Let me tell you the good news first. Conker's eye isn't nearly as bad as it looks. When Mr. Deans examined him he opened the wound and scraped out a lot of hardened pus."

"That sounds painful," Liz said, squirming.

"Better out than in," said Sophie. "The wound had swollen because of the infection and that was why his eye was closed. But when Mr. Deans examined the eye fully, it reacted to a beam of light."

"So Conker isn't blind on that side?" said David.

"No," said Sophie, taking a sandwich. "On Tuesday, Mr. Deans put two small stitches over the cut and gave Conker some antibiotics to prevent any more infections from developing. It healed very quickly; wounds like that often do."

David nodded and put her tea on the table. "So, if that was the good news, what's the bad?"

Sophie crossed her legs and twiddled a silver ring on her finger. Her voice dropped to a gentle murmur. "The rest has to do with the twitching you saw. Mr. Deans took a sample of Conker's blood and ran some tests on it. We had to wait for the results. That's why it took so long to get back to you."

David slipped into the chair beside Lucy's. Lucy had suddenly gotten very quiet.

Sophie looked at everyone in turn. "Conker has kidney failure," she whispered.

David stared at her for several seconds. "You mean he's going to die?"

"Yes."

Lucy immediately fell against her mother.

David looked away briefly, reached for a sandwich, then changed his mind. "How long does he have?"

"That's difficult to tell," Sophie said gently, looking sympathetically at Lucy. "There's no real way of knowing. Mr. Deans says he might live a long time . . . then again, he might not."

"He can't die," wailed Lucy. "Conker can't *die*."

David gulped and rubbed a hand across his mouth.

"I know it's sad," Sophie continued, "but try to think of it like this: If it hadn't been for you, Conker might not be alive today. You've given him the chance to live a lot longer. He's bouncing around very happily right now."

Lucy sniffed and wiped her eyes. "Can he go to the library gardens?"

Sophie smiled and cradled her tea in her hands. "Rosehip with milk. How unusual," she said. She braced herself and took a quick sip. "Well, that brings me to the other news."

David threw her a worried look.

"There was something else that Mr. Deans said. I didn't know before, but it seems gray squirrels are classed as pests."

Lucy's mouth fell open in shock. "Who said that? Was it Mr. Bacon?"

"Lucy, Lucy, shush," Liz soothed her.

"What are you saying?" David asked bluntly.

Sophie took a breath and came to the point. "By

law, if you catch a gray squirrel, you're not supposed to return it to the wild."

"*What?*" The pyramid of tuna sandwiches collapsed as David jarred a knee against the table top.

Liz frowned at him and popped a few back onto the plate. "You mean Conker *can't* leave the hospital, Sophie?"

"No!" Lucy shouted. "Conker wants to go to the *library gardens!*"

"And what about Snigger?" David rapped. "You can't keep him locked up."

Sophie fidgeted in her seat. She coughed and tugged at the hem of her skirt. "I thought you'd feel like this," she said slowly, "which makes what I have to say more bearable — I hope." The kitchen fell deathly quiet. Sophie stuck her chin in the air. "Some species of wild animals are very hard to keep. They gnaw at their cages or burrow in the earth. We have to be watchful or they find a way out."

"Find a way *out?*" There was rising anger in David now.

"Are you telling us Snigger escaped?" asked Liz.

Sophie pushed her hands between her thighs.

"Oh, no. I don't *believe* that!" David shouted. He thumped the table and rose to his feet. "I *told* you to watch him. I *told* you he was tricky."

Lucy, grasping at a thread of hope, said: "He's going back to the gardens, Mom!"

"He'll need a really good map if he is," said Liz. "It took me ages to find that hospital." She glared at David as he paced the kitchen.

"We've got to do something, quickly," he fretted. "He'll head across country, staying close to woodland, probably guided by the sun's position. He'll —"

"David, please. I haven't finished." Sophie tightened her lip. "They did get out —"

"What, *both* of them?"

"— yes, through a hole in the fence."

David threw up his hands in horror. "I'll get my coat. We've got to start looking for them, right away."

That was enough for Sophie. "Oh, David, *sit down!*"

243

The tenant stumbled back as if he couldn't quite believe the force of the reprimand. Even Liz raised a rather surprised (or possibly, impressed) eyebrow. David took his heel out of Bonnington's food dish — and sat.

Sophie pinned him with a steady stare. "Like I said, they *did* get out — but they didn't get far. I made sure of that."

"How?" asked Lucy.

Sophie bit into a sandwich and chewed it fast. "I was waiting for them on the other side."

David cocked his head. "Waiting? How?"

"Just *waiting*, David — with a small cat carrier."

Lucy looked open-mouthed at her mom.

"Oh, Sophie," sighed Liz, figuring out what she did.

Sophie's cheeks turned a delicate shade of red.

"You mean . . . you *caught* them?" Lucy asked.

"Yes," said Sophie, sipping her tea.

David's face went through a sea of expressions. He finally settled on "calm but intrigued." "Where is this carrier?"

"In the back of my car."

"Yes!" squealed Lucy, launching into a Sophie-sized hug.

"Gosh," said David, partly in shock, partly in admiration. He steepled his fingers around his nose.

Liz shook her head and rolled her eyes skyward. "Oh, Sophie," she sighed again.

DECISION TIME

"I want to see them!" Lucy declared. She stood up straight, beaming like a lighthouse. "But I have to go to the bathroom, first!" She tightened her fists and stomped from the kitchen.

"Right," said Liz. "While madam's out of the way, what's the plan for these squirrels?"

Sophie looked to David for a lead.

Leaning back against the counter, he said, "I think Lucy's right about the library gardens."

"I agree," said Sophie. "Conker will struggle in natural woodland."

"And if we let him go here," David continued, "there's no food, and he's in danger of encountering

246

Henry and the crow. The gardens are quiet. People feed the squirrels all the time. It's as good a place as any; better than most."

Sophie gave an encouraging nod.

"Right," said Liz. "Gardens it is. And if my daughter ends up with a criminal record, I'm doubling your rent, young man."

"Thanks," David snorted.

"You're welcome," said Liz. "We'll take my car."

On the drive into Scrubbley, Sophie said to David, "Tell me about this story you're writing?"

"It's brilliant," piped Lucy, twisting around in the passenger seat. "It's about how David went to the gardens and the squirrels thought he was a nutbeast because he stole their acorns and Snigger followed him home and —"

"Breathe," said Liz, pulling up at some lights.

Lucy breathed in. "— got trapped in the nutbox by mistake!"

"So it's true?"

David wiggled his fingers. "Based on truth." He adjusted his knees to keep the cat carrier as level as possible in his lap.

"He's been writing it down — for Lucy," said Liz, steering the car down Main Street. "Turning it into a real story."

"Gosh," said Sophie, arching an eyebrow. "You must have a wonderful imagination."

"Not really," said David with a shrug of modesty.

"That's right," Lucy added. "Gadzooks does it all."

"No, he doesn't," the tenant snapped back.

Sophie looked puzzled. "Who's Gadzooks?"

"David's dragon," said Lucy. "Mom made him a special story-writing one."

Liz caught Sophie's eye in the mirror. "I'm a potter; I make clay dragons."

"*Pennykettle Pots and Crafts*," said David.

Sophie thought for a moment, then her face lit up. "Not those spiky-winged dragons at Scrubbley Market?"

"Yes," said David and Lucy together.

"Oh, but they're *lovely*. I keep meaning to buy one, but I never have the money. Do you have a shop somewhere?"

"Just a studio, at home."

"The Dragons' Den," said Lucy.

"Entrance by invitation only," muttered David.

"I'll show you around later, if you like," said Liz.

Sophie glowed with delight. "Oh, yes, please. The Dragons' Den. Raar!"

"Actually, it's more like *hrrr!*" said David.

Liz flashed him a look in the rearview mirror.

For no apparent reason, David jerked in his seat as if he'd been stung. The carrier bounced on his knee, bringing forth a chatter of annoyance from within.

"What's the matter?" asked Sophie, looking him up and down.

David shook his head. "Nothing. I'm fine."

He peered at the rearview mirror again. Liz's eyes were back on the road. But in that moment he'd held her gaze, there was no mistaking what he'd seen. Her normally vivid pale green eyes had sparkled a very different color.

Violet.

Just like the dragon he had seen in his dream.

BYE-BYE, CONKER

Two minutes later the car was parked and the talk had turned to squirrels again.

"Come on, Mom," Lucy was saying. "We need to find a good place to let them out." She grabbed Liz's hand and pulled her along the library path.

Sophie laughed softly, watching them go. "They're a funny pair, aren't they?"

"You can say that again," David muttered, switching the carrier to his other hand; two active squirrels were surprisingly heavy.

Sophie turned and walked backward a step. "Don't you like being their tenant?"

"Yeah, they're great. They're just . . . weird —

251

especially when it comes to dragons. When we were in the car just now, did you see Liz's eyes change color?"

Sophie gave him a questioning look.

"Honest. I saw it in the mirror. They're normally green, but I saw them go violet."

Sophie sighed wistfully and tightened her scarf. "Lucky Liz. Wish mine did that; they do go bluer, in the right light."

"This was different," said David, shaking his head. "She went all 'dragony' for a moment."

"Hrrr," breathed Sophie, laughing as she blew warm air into her hands.

"I'm serious. There's something odd about those two. When we get home, ask Lucy to show you Gwendolen — that's one of her special dragons. If you stare at it closely, you can see Lucy in it."

"So?"

"Well . . . sometimes, when I look at Lucy, I think I see it the other way round. It's just as if —"

"Stop, there!" Lucy reappeared ten yards ahead, at a hairpin bend in the path. "Go closer," she shouted.

"And don't make a face." She brought her birthday camera to her eye.

"Oh no, not photos," Sophie winced. "I *always* make a face." She slipped her arm inside David's and smiled painfully.

There was a click. Lucy immediately shouted, "Mom, I took a picture of David and Sophie snuggling up!"

Liz's voice floated back. "I'm sure they'll treasure it all their lives. Come on, I found a good place."

David and Sophie "unsnuggled" themselves and followed Lucy along the path. They found Liz sitting on an ivy-covered wall, looking through a gap in the cluster of trees. The pond, with the bandstand away to its left, was framed at the bottom like a picture postcard. In the distance, just visible, was the wishing fountain.

"This is good," said Sophie, sitting down beside Liz. "Scrubby and woodsy. Lots of places to bury acorns."

"Speaking of which," David popped the carrier down on the path and took a bagful of acorns from his pocket. "Here, you can be nut monitor," he said, dumping them into Lucy's hands.

"Brilliant," said Lucy. "These are the ones he stole," she told Sophie.

David half knelt beside the carrier. "Well, now it's time to give them back — and to let Conker see his new home."

For the first time, Lucy looked a little glum. "Do we really have to let him go?"

David nodded at the carrier door. Snigger was clinging tightly to the mesh, doing his best to gnaw through the catch.

Lucy's bottom lip began to buckle. She stepped forward into David's arms and let her head fall against his shoulder. "Thank you for saving him."

David gave her a squeezy hug. "We all saved him, silly. You, me, your mom, Bonnington."

"Sophie," said Liz.

"Snigger," said Sophie.

"Gadzooks," sniffed Lucy. "He helped a lot."

"We'll have mentioned everyone in Scrubbley in a minute," muttered Liz. She raised an eyebrow in the hope of moving things along.

"Come on," said David, steering Lucy to the box, "you do the honors, just like before."

Lucy paused and looked at Sophie. "Conker won't die today, will he?"

Sophie tugged on the ends of her scarf. "No."

"OK," said Lucy. She bent down and quickly released the catch.

With one light bounce, Snigger was out. Two flicks of his pepper-colored tail took him to the opposite side of the path. He skipped through the black hooped railings and bounced a little way down the muddy embankment, pausing, feet splayed, to peer at the trees. His tail flicked out like a puff of gray smoke.

Conker, meanwhile, was still huddled up at the back of the carrier, showing no visible sign of emerging.

"Should I tip him out?" David asked Sophie.

"Throw in a nut," she suggested.

Lucy rolled one in front of the carrier.

Conker twitched as the acorn clacked against the plastic, but he still refused to budge. To make matters worse, competition had arrived. An inquisitive squirrel had just scrambled down the trunk of a tree and was edging up the path toward the group. It hopped fearlessly over David's foot, poked its nose briefly into the carrier, twitched with surprise at the sight of Conker, found the acorn, twirled it and ate it on the spot.

"Try again," said David.

Lucy dipped into the bag. "Mom, that might be Shooter," she whispered, nodding at the eating squirrel.

"It might be Snigger's Aunt Mabel, for all we know," said Liz. "Come on, throw some nuts."

Lucy let a handful tumble down the path.

Within minutes, she was handing out more. Snigger and "Shooter" both took acorns. While they were busy burying them, two more squirrels arrived. One appeared at Liz's back, sniffing at the fur of her sheepskin coat. The other, a sleek-looking creature with a tail like a fountain (whom Lucy vowed was certainly Cherrylea), came so close that Sophie was able to feed it by hand. Suddenly, squirrels were popping up everywhere. In the midst of it all, Conker hopped out of the carrier.

Bewildered by the hubbub going on around him, he scrambled to the refuge of a nearby boulder and huddled up against it, tail laid flat.

David tapped a worried foot.

"Don't fret," said Sophie. "I've released lots of animals back into the wild. They often take time to settle. Ooh, gosh, look at that one."

David followed her gaze. An extremely large squirrel had just appeared on a tree root right behind Conker's boulder. With a deftness that seemed to defy its bulk, it leapt onto the stone and looked down on Conker with a curious eye.

"It's Birchwood!" gasped Lucy.

"That's the one that chased Snigger from the fountain," said David.

Birchwood dropped onto the path, making Conker *chirr* in alarm.

"No!" said Sophie, holding David back. "You mustn't interfere. Conker has to learn to fend for himself."

"Against *him?*" David tightened a fist as Birchwood leaned forward to sniff Conker's tail.

"Sophie's right," said Liz. "You can't always be here." She prodded Lucy. "Throw Birchwood an acorn."

Lucy bowled the last one down the path. To her anguish, it twirled well past the big squirrel and wedged beneath the boulder, nearer to Conker.

Conker lowered his head to investigate.

"No, don't go for it," David muttered, convinced that Birchwood would launch an attack.

Which he did — but not against Conker. Another squirrel came forward to steal the nut . . . and Birchwood turned on *that* one instead.

"Hhh!" squealed Lucy, as Birchwood chased the other squirrel through her legs. The remaining squirrels scattered into the trees.

Birchwood returned to the path in triumph. He took up his position on the boulder again and let Conker eat his acorn in peace.

"How extraordinary," said Liz, taking a picture. "It appears that Conker has found a champion."

"That's bizarre," said David, sinking down onto the wall. "I've been trying for weeks to think of a way that Birchwood could turn out to be a hero in my story and . . . I just had a great idea. If I were at the computer now, I know who Birchwood would be."

"Who?" said Lucy.

David flicked a twig into the cluster of trees. "Conker's dad."

HELLO, GRUFFEN

Y ou have to write it down," Lucy insisted, pestering David all the way back to the car. "Chapter Nine. *Conker's Dad.* You can do it as soon as we get back home."

"Thank you very much," David said dryly.

"Lucy, give it a rest," said her mom. She pressed a button in the center of her key fob. The locks on the car popped up with a clunk.

"Why did Birchwood leave the Crescent?" Lucy chattered. "Why didn't he stay and save Conker from Caractacus?"

"I know," said Sophie, putting up a hand. "Male squirrels have nothing to do with their young. The mother raises them all on her own. A bit like you and . . ."

Her words trailed away into an awkward silence.

"Oh dear, I'm almost out of gas," said Liz, as if she hadn't heard a thing.

But Lucy had. "You mean like Mom and me?"

Sophie blushed profusely and fiddled with her seat belt.

"One more from the princess of subtlety," sighed Liz. "Perhaps Birchwood is just a New Age dad. A squirrel for the new millennium."

David clipped on his seatbelt and said, "More likely he just recognized Conker's scent. This time next week, I bet Birchwood will be chasing Conker around like he does with all the other squirrels."

"I'm coming back next week," smiled Lucy.

"Excuse me?" said her mom.

"You said we could."

"I most certainly did not."

"You most certainly *did*. When Conker and

Birchwood hopped off toward the duck pond and I was waving and crying on your coat and David was holding Sophie's hand —" (there was a rustle of movement in the back of the car as David and Sophie pressed themselves against their respective windows) "— you said we could come back and see him again."

"I didn't say next week."

"Hmph," went Lucy. "Well, I'm going to come back *secretly* and build my own treehouse and live here forever — up a big tree!"

"Fine. I'll help you pack."

"Good," Lucy gibbered, crossing her arms. "Just make sure you remember my pajamas!"

In the time it took to return to the Crescent, Lucy had tired of the treehouse idea ("no TV," David assured her) and was focusing all her attention instead on the promise of a tour around the Dragons' Den, for Sophie.

"I'll show you," she said, grabbing Sophie's hand as they entered the house.

"Lucy, wait for me," Liz said. She took off her coat and fluffed her hair.

Lucy tapped an impatient foot. She was halfway up the stairs with Sophie already.

David hovered at the bottom, saying nothing. On the ride home, he'd been thinking hard about "dragony" things: Liz's eye color, Lucy's likeness to Gwendolen, the burning doorknob, the story of Gawain, the ever-present *hrring* noises. He had not been inside the dragons' "lair" since the day he retrieved the hutch from the attic. Three days ago the kilning sign was removed from the door. And though he had inquired about the progress of Gawain and been told by a clear-voiced, chirpy Lucy: "He's better. Can't you *tell?*" no one had invited him to see the special dragon. Now was his chance for a good look around. And this time, he wasn't going to waste it.

With Liz's go-ahead, Lucy bounded upstairs. She and Sophie disappeared (unscathed) into the den. Liz followed. David dawdled on the threshold. He waited till Liz and Lucy weren't looking, then racked the doorknob left and right.

Normal.

"Oh, wow," Sophie gushed, overwhelmed by the rows of spiky creations. "Look at this one. And this. And this *baby*, hatching from its egg."

Lucy turned to her mom. "Can Sophie have one?"

"I'd love one," said Sophie. "How much are they?"

"Oh, don't be silly," said Liz, flapping a hand. "Have a look around. If any of them speak to you —"

Suddenly, there was a clunk from the back of the room. Everyone turned to see David on his knees, rubbing the back of his head.

"David, what are you doing?" said Liz.

David flushed with guilt. He didn't think "looking for an oven" would be the sort of answer Liz would want to hear. "Um, slipped on some clay; banged my head on a shelf getting up."

Liz looked down at the polished boards. There wasn't a smidgen of clay to be seen. She turned again to Sophie. "As I was saying, just choose one you like, and it's yours."

"Except for them." Lucy pointed to the bench.

Sophie puttered across the room to investigate a dragon on the potter's wheel. "He's fierce," she said.

"That's Gawain," said Lucy, swelling with pride. "I broke him last week. He's just been mended."

Sophie turned the wheel a few degrees either way. "You'd never know."

You wouldn't, thought David, peering over Sophie's shoulder. Liz had done a remarkable job. Gawain was standing with his veined wings tented and every claw spread neatly to a sharpened point. If anything, he looked more threatening than ever. As Sophie returned the wheel to rest, the dragon was suddenly lit from behind in a halo of rays from the setting sun. David almost jumped onto the nearest shelf. His first impression had been to think that the dragon had actually burst into flames. He sighed at his stupidity and glanced at the window. On the sill were several pieces of plywood, which looked as if they might have clay stains on them. Maybe *that* was Liz's kilning secret? Perhaps she baked her sculptures in sunlight?

"Who's this?" asked Sophie, moving on.

"Guinevere," said Lucy, lowering her voice. "She's Mom's special dragon."

"Is she praying?" Sophie steepled her fingers, mimicking Guinevere's virtuous pose.

Lucy shook her head and whispered into Sophie's ear.

"Making fire?" Sophie exclaimed quietly.

"What?" said David, turning in surprise. He knocked a knee against the workbench, upsetting a jar of brushes and sticks.

Liz righted them and said, "David, behave, or you'll have to leave."

"But Lucy said Guinevere was making fire."

Lucy stepped behind her mother to avoid eye contact.

"They *are* dragons," laughed Sophie. "What do you expect?"

"Right," said Liz, frowning at the tenant. She guided Sophie toward another shelf.

David hung back to look closely at Guinevere. The red-haired girl from the dragon story had never really come up in his thoughts before. Why did she have a dragon named after her? A special one at that. David stared hard at the sculpture.

And saw Elizabeth Pennykettle in it.

Suddenly, he found himself thinking back to Sophie's *faux pas* in the car. If Guinevere was Liz, and Gwendolen was Lucy, did that then mean that Gawain was . . . ? David stared into the fiery eyes. . . .

One second, two seconds, three seconds, four . . .

All he saw was a dragon.

No more.

"This one's sweet," Sophie piped up.

David glanced across the room and saw Sophie reach out for a fragile-looking creature with angelic wings and shell-like ears. She took it off the shelf, then paused for a second. Her head leaned forward slightly. "Hello, who's that — hiding in the back?"

"Ah," said Liz, reaching forward. She pulled a youthful-looking dragon to the front of the shelf. "That's Gruffen. He's not for giving away either, I'm afraid."

Gruffen. A spark lit up in David's mind.

"He shouldn't be on this shelf," said Liz. "Lucy, put Gruffen in his proper place, would you?"

Lucy took Gruffen to the shelf by the door. "Stay there and don't be so naughty," she muttered.

"Oh dear, poor Gruffen," Sophie laughed. "He has lovely eyes, doesn't he? Soppy, like a puppy."

"What?" grunted David. Somewhere at the back of his mind a dreamlike image roared to life — of a soppy-looking dragon with violet eyes, framed in the shape of a tiny keyhole. He swept across the room to investigate Gruffen.

"What's the matter with you now?" said Liz.

"It's him," gasped David, staring Gruffen in the face. "I had a really weird dream when Gawain got broken — all about a dragon, guarding this room. It had violet eyes and it looked like him."

"His eyes are green," said Sophie.

"Yeah, but — hang on, what's that he's standing on?"

"His book," huffed Lucy as if anyone with eyes to see could tell.

Gruffen was perched on a hardback book made entirely from clay.

"I don't remember seeing that before," said David.

"You wouldn't; I only just made it," said Liz.

David moved Gruffen and picked up the book. "Can't open it."

Sophie whispered in his ear: "I think that's because it's made of clay." She held up the dragon with the shell-like ears. "I'll take this one, if I may."

"She's a listening dragon," Lucy said. "You can tell her things. What will you call her?"

"Let's decide over a cup of tea," said Liz. "Come along, David, *you* can put the kettle on." And exchanging quiet words about people with overactive imaginations, she and Sophie left the den.

Lucy folded her arms and waited for David.

"You can't hide it from me forever," he said,

plunking Gruffen back on his book. "I dreamed about that dragon. I *know* it was him." *Hrrr!* he went, in Gruffen's face.

"You shouldn't have done that," Lucy bristled.

David thumbed his nose and turned away.

As he did there came a gentle *hrrr* from behind. "Ow!" he exclaimed, clapping a hand to the back of his neck. "What was that? Something . . . *burned* me."

"Serves you right," said Lucy, pushing him out. "You shouldn't mess around when their eyes are lit."

"Lit?" said David, glancing back. Lucy was quickly shutting the door. The gap narrowed and narrowed, shutting Gruffen out of sight. But it was open long enough for David to glimpse one single, sparkling, violet eye.

SNOOP

Sophie named her dragon Grace.

"Very apt," said Liz.

"I like it," said Lucy.

"It's not very magical," David grumbled.

"Ignore him, he's in a funny mood," said Liz.

Sophie turned her wrist and glanced at her watch. "It's time for me to go. Thank you for the tea — and Grace; she's lovely. I've had a super day. I'm glad I was able to help with the squirrels."

Lucy threw her arms around Sophie's waist. "You will come back again, won't you?"

"I'd love to," said Sophie. "When you go and visit Conker, I'll come along too — if that's all right?"

"Oh, I hope we see you before then," said Liz, prodding a finger into David's back.

"Um, what? Oh, I'll walk you to your car," he said.

As they stepped outside into the cold, crisp air, Sophie was the first to speak. "What was all that about in the den? You were acting really weird." She put Grace on the roof of the car and rummaged around in her bag for her keys.

"There are things going on in this house," said David. "Odd, *unworldly* things."

"You're not telling me you're hearing bumps in the night?"

"No, growls in the night."

Sophie's mouth twitched into a grin. "David, all houses make peculiar noises. Ours creaks and bloggles and gloops all the time."

"Yeah, I know, but they're normal noises. This one *hrrrs*. Liz says it's the central heating, but she doesn't have any radiators."

Sophie gave it a moment's thought. "I guess it's the dragons snoring."

David threw up his hands in despair.

"Well, what do *you* think it is?" she laughed, throwing her bag onto the passenger seat.

"Don't know," he said, resting on the hood. "But they're keeping *something* secret. It all has to do with Liz's glazing process. She keeps making these dragons, but she hasn't got a kiln. How can she fire them without an oven?"

"Perhaps she doesn't need to," Sophie said, shrugging. "Maybe she uses a special kind of clay?"

David shook his head. "She heats them somehow. While she was mending Gawain she put a sign on the den saying 'KILNING — NO ENTRY'. I tried to sneak in to see what was happening, but when I touched the doorknob it burned my hand."

"Serves you right," Sophie said primly. "That was your conscience trying to warn you."

"No, it was *Gruffen*, keeping guard. He flamed the handle when I tried to turn it. Just now upstairs, when I breathed on him, he scorched my neck. Take a look if you don't believe me. There must be a mark."

Sophie frowned and took a look. "All I can see is a spot the size of Everest."

"A spot?" said David, feeling for it.

"Yeah. How's this for a burning sensation?" Sophie breathed on it, making him wince. "I think you'll find it was Lucy who *hrred*. Speaking of whom . . ." She tilted her head toward the house. Lucy was standing in the front room window, waving and pulling a smoochy face.

David stuck out his tongue.

"Hey, be nice to her," Sophie clucked. "She's going to need you now. Life will be quiet without the squirrels. She'll miss them. So will you."

David folded his arms and shrugged.

"At least you've got the story," Sophie continued. "That should keep both of you happy. *Conker's Dad*. That's the next chapter, isn't it?"

"No," David said firmly. "It's 'Conker went to the library gardens, lived happily ever after and the nutbeast was never pestered by the little girl again. The End.' I'm going to write it tonight and give it to her tomorrow. Then it's 'really' finished, as she likes to say."

Sophie smiled and got into her car, throwing an empty potato chip bag off the seat. "I hope Conker lives a good while. I think if I were Lucy's age it would be sweet to read about him enjoying himself in the library gardens, even if I knew he was ultimately going to kick the bucket."

"No worries about that," David grunted. "I'm under strict instructions to write a happy ending. Rule number 97: You're not allowed to make a dragon cry."

"Right," said Sophie, starting the engine. "Tears might quench their fire."

"Go away," David sighed. "You're as bad as they are."

"Thank you. I will now go home and sulk."

The tenant grimaced and chewed his lip. "I didn't mean it. I was only teasing. You will come back again — won't you?"

"Possibly," said Sophie, turning her cheek.

David took a breath. Was this an invitation to kiss her good-bye? He said a quick prayer and puckered his lips . . .

. . . just as Lucy pounded up the driveway. "Stop!"

"Oh, Lucy! What —? OW!" David bellowed, banging his nose on the frame of the door.

"Grace," she cried, pointing.

"Hhh!" gasped Sophie. "She's still on the roof!"

Grumbling, David snatched her down.

Lucy took her and handed her to Sophie. "She didn't like it when the car went *vroom*. She thought you were going away without her."

"No way," Sophie whistled. "Thanks, Luce."

"Yes, *thanks,* Lucy," David added. "You can go inside again now."

"I'm staying here, waving bye-bye," she said, resisting all attempts to be shoved aside.

"Don't fight," said Sophie. "I'll see you both soon." She blew both of them a kiss and reversed down the driveway. The car roared away in a cloud of blue smoke.

As it disappeared around the Crescent, Lucy swung her hips and said to David, "Did you mean it? Will you really finish *Snigger* tonight?"

"Possibly. I'll — hang on. How did *you* know I might do the story tonight?"

Lucy's face turned fire-engine red.

"You were snooping," David accused her. "You had that window open, didn't you? You shouldn't listen in on private conversations."

"I didn't!"

"Don't lie. It just makes things worse."

Lucy stamped an indignant foot. "I wasn't listening in on your *private conversations*."

David glared at her and walked away.

"I wasn't!" she shouted. "Don't you *dare* tell Mom!"

David wagged a finger. "You were listening. Don't deny it."

"I *wasn't*," Lucy said again, almost in tears. She kicked a stone along the driveway. "Grace was."

THE FINAL WORDS

As a punishment, David didn't complete the story that night. Or the next. Or the next. Or the one after that. No amount of pestering could make him type a word. Lucy told him she hated him more than cold oatmeal. He replied that her nose would grow for telling lies and threatened to *stir* his oatmeal with it. Lucy said she'd tear the story up and throw it in the trash. David said, Fine, it was in the computer anyway.

It took a phone call from Sophie to turn things around. "Don't be mean," she said when she learned what was happening. "I don't remember the windows being open. How could she have heard us? Write the story — or I'll set Gruffen on you."

278

The hairs rose on the back of David's neck.

He decided to end the feud.

The following evening, he was lying on the sofa watching TV when Lucy slipped into the room. She was wearing her pajamas and bathrobe.

"I found this under my pillow." She flapped two sheets of paper at him.

"Gosh, that squirrel fairy is quick," he said. (Lucy had visited the dentist that day.)

"I read it."

"I gathered. Did you like it?"

Lucy shuffled her feet and flopped into a chair. "When are you going to write some more?"

David threw her a glance. "There isn't any more. They're the last two pages."

"You mean this is it?" She held up a page and started to read: "*For the rest of that week, the library gardens were alive with the drama of the nutbeast.*"

"Lu-cy."

"*Snigger told his story so many times that he couldn't remember who'd heard it and who hadn't and received*" *several dark looks from irritated squirrels who all seemed to have a drey to build."*

David turned up the TV sound.

Lucy turned up her voice: "*Snigger could not remember a time when there had been so much construction work going on, but at least it reminded him of the urgent need to find Conker somewhere to sleep. So, joining forces with Ringtail and Birchwood, he began to search out a good place for Conker's new home."*

"Lucy, buzz off. I know what I wrote."

"*Taking into careful consideration Conker's climbing difficulties, they opted for a hollow in the trunk of an ash. The ash stood next to a notice-board, supported from the ground by two metal legs and a sloping wooden strut. The strut was a perfect approach to the tree. In no time at all, Conker was able to reach his hollow without any fears of falling."*

"I'm not listening."

"*And so it was that the little squirrel settled into his brand-new home and lived a happy and contented life. The End."*

"Thank you. Can I watch soccer now?"

Lucy found the remote control and muted the sound.

David gave her a very hard stare. "What's wrong with that ending?"

"It's not very *interesting*, is it?"

"It's not meant to be 'interesting'. It's supposed to be happy."

"But nothing *happens*. It ends too soon."

David threw up his hands. "There's nothing else to write."

"There is," said Lucy, widening her eyes. "You can write about Conker's adventures in the gardens!"

"No chance," David snorted. "That's another book entirely."

"Yes!"

"No! One story was enough."

For once, Lucy knew that the tenant meant it. "Well, finish this one the right way, then. Ask Gadzooks, he'll know what to do."

"I'm perfectly capable of writing it myself."

Lucy gave him a doubtful look.

David groaned and snatched up the manuscript. "All right, I'll ask the dragon!"

He got to work on it the following Sunday afternoon. "Okay," he muttered, firing up the computer. "This is it. The final words." He grabbed Gadzooks while the screen was clearing. "Sharpen your pencil and clear your pad. We're finishing this today."

Gadzooks chewed the end of his pencil in silence.

"No, wait," David said, plunking him down. "I'll do it myself. I'll show her."

And he started to type.

Then erase.

Then type.

Then cut.

Then mutter.

Then fiddle with the mouse.

Then mutter some more.

After fifteen minutes on one short sentence he stood up and started to pace the room.

"This is stupid," he groaned, running a hand through his hair in frustation. "All I want is a nice, happy, believable ending." Sighing loudly, he turned to the window. Outside, in the garden, shadows rolled across the empty lawn. *What's really happening at the library?* he wondered. He closed his eyes and tried to imagine. Without prompting, Gadzooks wrote a word on his pad.

Nine

It appeared slowly, letter by letter, as if it had been an effort to write.

"Nine?" David queried. "Can't be Chapter Nine, I wrote that." With one finger, he typed the letters. N . . . I . . . N . . . E.

Then added another word to it . . . BONGS.

Nine bongs. Doom and gloom.

A horrible feeling began to creep over him. A strange unnerving realization of what Gadzooks was trying to say. David sat back and stared at the ceiling.

"No," he whispered, "I can't write that." He waved his hands in front of the dragon. "No, anything but that."

At that moment, Sophie entered the room. "Hiya," she announced, knocking gently. She walked her fingers over David's shoulders and left a feather-light kiss on his head. "Came a bit early 'cause I had to take the bus." She glanced at the screen. "Ooh, nine bongs. Spooky."

David switched the computer off.

"Hey, it's OK," Sophie said, prodding him. "Go on, if you're in the middle of something. I'll go and have a cup of tea with Liz. I wouldn't want to come between a man and his dragon."

"Don't feel like writing," David said tautly.

"Aah, poor Zookie," Sophie simpered. "He looks all crestfallen now."

"Sophie, he's made of clay," David snapped. "He can't look any different from the way he always does."

"Yawch, OK, Mr. Bear. I'll come back when you're not so grumpy."

"Wait. I'm sorry." David held her arm. "I'm having a few problems with the story, that's all. I have a little headache, too. Would you like to take a walk? Fresh air helps."

Sophie nodded. "OK. Where?"

David raised his head and stared out the window. "How about the library gardens?"

THE
SPOTTING GAME

Great," said Sophie. "Let's all go."

"What?"

"To the gardens — all of us. I promised Lucy ages ago. She'll be terribly upset if she knows we went and didn't invite her."

"But —?"

Sophie jumped up and strolled toward the door. "I'll check with Liz. It'll be fun to go back and try to find Conker. That *was* what you had in mind — wasn't it?"

Half an hour later the four of them were walking down the library path when Liz said, "Is it me, or is someone sucking cough drops?"

"David's feeling a little under the weather," said Sophie.

"I've got a headache and a slight sore throat," he said.

"I bet it's dragon pox," Lucy diagnosed.

"What?" said Sophie.

"Our term for sneezes and sniffles," said Liz, casting a momentary glance at David. He sighed and looked away into the trees.

"Don't worry about him. I want to play a game." Lucy pulled a bag of mixed nuts from her pocket. "It's called the spotting game and these are the rules. The first person to see a squirrel is allowed to feed it . . . a peanut."

"What if it's way up a tree?" said her mom.

"Mom, you wait till it comes *down*, of course. And if someone *guesses* at a place and a squirrel is there, they're allowed to feed it a . . . what are these knobby ones called?"

"Walnuts," said Liz. "Come on, hurry up. It's chilly, standing around."

Sophie clapped her gloved hands together and said, "I guess the wall where we let Conker go."

"It's not your turn," Lucy frowned. "I made up the game. I have to start. I guess . . . the wall where we let Conker go!"

And she turned and scooted down the path.

Half a minute later the adults caught up. Lucy was sitting on the wall, idly swinging her feet.

"Any luck?" asked Sophie.

"No," came the rather glum reply. "I wouldn't have picked this spot if you hadn't said to."

Sophie laughed and threw a length of scarf across her shoulder. "OK, you can have my turn."

"OK," said Lucy, jumping to her feet. Her ponytail bumped against the hood of her coat. She pulled up her socks and narrowed her gaze. "I guess . . . the wishing fountain."

"Race you to it," said Sophie. And together they skittered down a track through the trees, Lucy squealing with delight all the way.

"Oh, to have such energy," said Liz. She looped her

arm through David's and tugged him closer. "How long have you had this throat infection?"

"It's nothing. Don't fuss. I'm fine."

"OK, but you're very quiet. It's almost as if you'd rather not be here."

David shrugged and looked away. "I feel a little weird coming back, that's all."

Before Liz could comment, they heard Lucy shout: "Mom! Mom! Down here, quick!"

"Sounds like she spotted one," David said. He uncoupled himself from Liz's arm and hurried away before she could stop him.

As it happened, Lucy had not seen a squirrel — she'd found a horse chestnut tree instead. When David arrived, he had to wade through a sea of chestnuts to reach her.

"Look," said Lucy, resting a spiky green shell in her palm. She put her thumbnail into a split and pried the shell open. A shiny brown nut gleamed out like a jewel. "I'm going to feed this to Conker."

"He'll only spit it out if you do," said Sophie. "I think chestnuts are poisonous to squirrels."

David flinched and closed his eyes.

"What's the matter?" asked Sophie, feeling him shudder. She removed a glove and pressed a hand against his brow. "You're warm. I think you're running a temperature."

"Dragon pox makes you warm," said Lucy. "And grumpy — doesn't it, Mom?"

"I don't have *dragon pox*," David said gruffly, pushing away before Liz could get involved. "Are we going to the wishing fountain or not?"

Sophie caught up with him and poked him in the ribs. "Hey, what's with the tantrum? You were the one who wanted to come out."

"Sorry," he whispered, close to her ear. "I just feel a little strange; I can't talk about it here." He shook his head as if banishing a cloud. "Let's go and see if Snigger is by the fountain."

But Snigger wasn't by the fountain.

They sat on the wall and waited for ages.

Lucy made a wish.

Sophie made another.

Liz produced a thermos of tea and some cookies. But even a shower of cookie crumbs, sprayed around the roots of the beech itself, couldn't drag a single squirrel into view.

It was the same at the bandstand.

And the great oak.

"Where *are* they?" Lucy pined, joining the others on the bench that circled the trunk of the tree.

"We could always try splitting up," said David.

"Splitting up?" said Lucy. "What does he mean?"

"I have no idea," said Sophie, looking puzzled and annoyed.

"If you two want to be alone . . . ?" said Liz.

"We don't," Sophie bristled. "We came here to-gether and we're staying together. I don't know what's gotten into David today. He's being very dull and bor-ing and gloomy." She snatched her hand away from his arm and pushed it into the pocket of her coat.

David tried to explain: "I just thought if we searched in pairs we'd have a better chance of spotting one, that's all."

"But that's not playing the game," said Lucy.

"No, it isn't," said Sophie. "Whose turn is it?"

"His."

Sophie swallowed a sigh. "Well? Where do you think?"

David picked at a button on his coat. "It's impossible to know. They could be anywhere."

"Maybe we should just go home," said Liz.

"No," said Sophie. "Not until David joins in the game." She stared at him darkly.

"All right," he said, covering his eyes. "I guess . . ." *Where?* he asked himself, and saw Gadzooks write:

George

on his pad. *Go away,* growled David, tightening his fist. *Just leave me alone, OK?* Gadzooks dropped his pencil and slowly disappeared. Even so, it didn't stop David from saying, ". . . the gardener's hut."

"Yes!" exclaimed Lucy, running around to stand in front of Sophie. "They go and steal the gardener's sandwiches sometimes!"

"A-ha," said Sophie. "No wonder they don't want our measly peanuts." She stood up and flicked a leaf at David. "Come on, Mr. Misery, you can lead the way."

He took them back to the duck pond. They followed the water around in an arc, passing through a corridor of weeping willows and a slippery patch of wild bird droppings, before climbing through several conifer beds, then out again onto level ground.

As they were passing a memorial stone, rising from the earth like a granite finger, the library clock began to strike.

David counted nine slow bongs. He stopped in his tracks as the others walked on.

Just ahead of them now was the gardener's hut, tucked away in a small enclosure framed by a waist-high hedge. At the rear of the hut was a mound of old cuttings. David sidled toward it as Lucy rapped her knuckles on the base of a wheelbarrow. The noise brought the gardener into the open.

"Aft'noon," he grunted. "Mrs. Pennykettle, isn't it?"

"Hello, George," said Liz, shaking hands. "Nice to see you again. How's Mrs. Digwell?"

"Still dustin' that dragon you sold her. It's got pride o' place on the mantelpiece, I tell you. What can I do for you?"

"This is my daughter, Lucy," said Liz, guiding her forward by the shoulders. "And our friend, Sophie. And David, our tenant . . . who seems to have disappeared for the moment. We were hoping to see some squirrels, George, but there don't seem to be many around today."

"Oh, they're around," George said frostily. "Diggin' in my roses all yest'day. To tell you the truth, Mrs. Pennykettle, I've only seen the one this mornin', over by the big horse ches'nut tree."

"We've been there," said Lucy.

"We didn't see one," Sophie added.

George ran a hand around his bristly chin. "Well, no, you wouldn't. The squirrel I saw ain't there anymore."

"How do you know?" asked Lucy.

George gave a backward tilt of his head. "I dropped it yonder not two hours since. Over there, where the boy is lookin' around."

Sophie shot a worried glance at David.

He looked up from the side of the mound. His eyes were staring and his face was pale. Slowly, he brought his hands into view. A still, gray body was lying across them.

It was Conker.

The little squirrel was dead.

NATURE'S WAY

Lucy quivered and her bottom lip started to shudder.

"Oh dear," said Liz, gathering her in her arms.

"He's dead," bawled Lucy. "Conker's *dead*."

David rested Conker in the crook of his arm and picked a seed pod out of the squirrel's tail.

"Sssh," Liz soothed, hugging Lucy tight. "We knew it would happen. We knew he was ill."

"But why did it have to happen today?"

"Oh heck," said George, looking rather bewildered. "I seem to have started a bit of somethin'. I'm sorry, Mrs. Pennykettle. Do you know this animal?"

"Yes," said Sophie, getting in first. She took a purse from her pocket and pulled out a card. "I'm a volunteer with the Wildlife Hospital. I'm involved in a project that's tracking the migration of gray squirrels from urban areas to woodland — I mean parkland — no, library land! These people are my helpers. This squirrel used to live in their garden."

George added another crease to his face. "You mean it's a sort of pet?"

"Yes," said Sophie, fighting back a tear.

"*Waah!*" wailed Lucy.

George shook his head and slid back his cap. "I know you, don't I?" he said to David.

David nodded. "I came here once to ask about squirrels. Would it be all right if we buried him, Mr. Digwell? Here, in the gardens? Anywhere . . . here?"

Liz gave George a plaintive look.

"Bear with me," he said, and popped into his hut. He emerged seconds later, tapping a trowel against his palm. "I dunno if it helps but I'm goin' to say it anyway: I've seen a lot of creatures die in these gardens and the way I always look at it is this . . ."

Liz turned Lucy around.

". . . these thievin' rascals," he nodded at Conker,

"will eat anythin' they can lay their graspin' paws on. Mostly they take from that oak in the clearin'. That big tree feeds them all their lives. But trees need feedin' too. They need to take nutrients out o' the ground." George looked kindly into Lucy's face. "It's not pleasant, I know, to think of your squirrel lyin' dead in the soil, but his body will help these trees survive. So I s'pose, by rights, he should be buried here. That way, he's doin' his pals a favor. What you take from the earth, you must give back. That's nature's way."

Liz put a hand on Lucy's brow. "I think we understand that, don't we?"

"Yes," said Lucy, with a little squeak.

"Ah, well, I'd best get back to work," said George. He nodded at Liz and tugged his cap, then handed the trowel to David. "Here, you'll be needin' this. Plant him where he can do some good."

At Sophie's suggestion they took Conker back to the horse chestnut tree. David laid him down around the back of the tree where the soil was dry and easier to dig in. With the tip of the trowel he traced a line around Conker's body then moved him aside and started to dig.

Lucy stroked Conker and talked to him constantly. She told him she loved him and always would. She chattered about the garden in Wayward Crescent, the felling of the oak tree, David coming, the drey in the roof, Mr. Bacon's trap, Caractacus's claw, the ongoing story of *Snigger and the Nutbeast* (the best birthday present ever, she said) and how everyone, Snigger especially, would miss him. David dug in time to her words, stabbing and scooping at the dark brown earth. He dug until the hole was as deep as his forearm and the sides were steep and smooth and square. When it was done he dropped the trowel and sat back on his heels, panting lightly.

"What now?" said Lucy.

David looked into her wide green eyes. "Now we have to put him to bed." And he picked Conker up, gently but securely, and lowered him into the ground.

One single green leaf fluttered into the hole.

David stood up, brushing down his coat, triggering a minor avalanche of soil.

Sophie crumpled, uncrumpled and recrumpled a tissue.

Lucy started to weep again.

"Don't be sad," said Liz. "Look how pretty and peaceful he is."

Conker's slim gray body lay curved across the grave, sort of like a miniature rainbow.

"Did anything hurt him?" Lucy asked, almost having to hiccup the words.

"No, I don't think so," David said quietly.

Lucy knelt down. She kissed one finger and touched it to the scar above Conker's eye. "He looks like he's sleeping — doesn't he, Mom?"

"Yes," said Liz. "He wuzzled off nicely."

David's blue eyes filmed with tears. He picked up the gardener's trowel and cleaned it doggedly with his thumb.

"Come on, let's tuck him in together," said Liz. She crouched down, scooped up a handful of soil and let it tumble into the grave.

Sophie hunkered down and joined in too. "Bye-bye, Conker. I hope this tree grows bigger and stronger with you beside it and brings happiness and joy to everyone who sees it." She squeezed Lucy's hand. Lucy threw in some soil.

Steadily, the hole began to fill, until there came a moment when Conker was almost completely covered and all that could be seen was the outline of his face. Lucy leaned back, not wanting to continue. She and Sophie both looked at David.

David found a suitable lump of soil and broke it slowly in his fist. Whispering a last good-bye, he moved his hand over Conker's body. The dry earth trickled through his fingers. *Pitter, patter.* Dust to dust. He shuddered and closed his eyes. When he opened them again, Conker was gone.

From that moment on, Lucy took over. With Sophie's help, she pushed the remaining soil into the grave and patted it down with her gloveless hands. While they were covering the site with underbrush, Liz drifted away to talk to David.

He was sitting alone on a low brick wall, rolling a dead leaf through his fingers.

"Are you OK?" Liz whispered, rubbing his arm.

"Not really," he said in a voice that carried the faint shudder of despair. "All I wanted was a happy ending. Now, I don't know what to do."

Liz sat down and covered his hand. "You could cry if you want to. That would be a start."

David gritted his teeth and looked away.

"No one's going to think you're a softy," Liz told him. "It won't help, you know, holding it in. Maybe Gadzooks —"

"I don't want to know about *Gadzooks!*" David stood up suddenly, throwing out a hand. "I'm fed up of hearing about your *stupid dragons!*" He waved the trowel in the air and turned away. "I have to take this to the gardener, OK?"

"What's happening?" said Sophie, hurrying over with Lucy. "What's going on? Where's David going? David, come back!" She started after him.

Lucy looked worriedly at her mom. "Why was he shouting about the dragons?"

Liz pulled a tissue out of her sleeve and did her best to clean Lucy's hands. "He's upset about Conker, and confused about the dragons. I think he is in a fight with Gadzooks."

Lucy's mouth fell open in shock. "Gadzooks won't make a fire tear, will he?"

Liz flicked a speck of soil off Lucy's bangs. "Gadzooks is a very proud young dragon. It would take a lot of shouting to put out his fire."

"But Mom, if David doesn't *love* him?"

"He does," Liz assured her, cleaning her face. "We might have to show him he does, that's all."

Lucy's eyes grew huge with astonishment. "Are you going to tell him about . . . y'know?"

"Only what he needs to know," said Liz. She touched a finger to Lucy's nose. "The rest he can dream for himself. After all, he's very good at making up stories, isn't he?"

DAVID RETURNS

David walked in at ten past six. Three hours had passed since his outburst in the gardens. He was shivering and his hair was dripping wet. The bottoms of his jeans were splattered with mud. One shoe was so soaked it squirted water over Bonnington as the cat came to greet him. When he hung up his coat, it fell off the hook. At the second attempt he sneezed so forcefully he sprayed half the mirror with the contents of his nostrils. By that time, Liz was in the doorway of the living room, arms folded, tapping her foot.

She said nothing to David, just "towel" to Lucy as Lucy came pounding downstairs to see.

Lucy asked no questions, just turned and went.

David swept his hair off his rain-soaked brow,

sending a rivulet of water down his nose. "Went for a walk," he said rather timidly.

"Through a car wash, by the look of it," Liz said, unimpressed.

Lucy reappeared with a large bath towel. As she handed it to David her mother said stiffly, "Dry your hair. Take off anything wet. Then wrap yourself up in your blanket, clothed. You need to warm yourself slowly. I'll make you a drink." She walked into the kitchen and plugged in the kettle.

David, knowing there was no point in arguing, squelched down the hall, toweling his hair.

"Should I call Sophie?" Lucy called to her mom.

David halted and looked at each of them.

"We took her home," Liz told him. "Tell her he's back," she shouted to Lucy, "and there's no need to call every half hour now." She gave David a critical look.

He shivered and went to his room.

Shortly afterward, Liz came in with a drink; something fruity, billowing steam. She put it on his desk and pulled the curtains half closed, reducing the room to a softer light. David, under the blanket as instructed, had Winston in his arms and Bonnington nestling at the foot of the bed.

"You're mad at me, aren't you?" he said.

Liz sat on the bed with her hands in her lap. "Concerned would be a better word. Getting soaked is bad enough at the best of times, but when you're not well and upset into the bargain . . ."

"I didn't mean about getting wet. I meant about what I said in the gardens. I'm sorry, I shouldn't have shouted like that."

"Sit up," said Liz. "Have your drink. It's honey and lemon. It'll help to clear your head."

David shuffled into a sitting position. He cupped the mug in his hands and took a few sips.

"You're a silly boy, sometimes," Liz said gently. "Why did you go stomping off like that? Why didn't you just stay and talk to me?"

David shook his head. "Don't know. It just happened." He put the mug down and sank back against his pillows, his head just clonking the wall. "When we buried Conker I was really mixed up; sad and bitter, all at the same time. It seemed so unfair that he would go and die after everything Lucy and I had done. The whole thing seemed so pointless."

Liz smoothed a crease in her skirt and said, "But can't you see how much you've achieved? You've brought joy and adventure to Lucy's life — and who knows what to the library gardens."

"Conker's still dead."

"No," said Liz. "He's alive in your story. And that's the greatest achievement of all. Conker helped you find something you never knew you had."

"Yeah, that I'm useless at writing stories." David thumped a fist against Winston's body, making the old bear baa like a sheep. "What can I do for Lucy now? How can I end the story happily, without, you know . . ."

"Fudging the truth?"

David sighed and ran a thumb down Winston's ear. "I spent ages in the gardens thinking about it. And before you say it, I did try asking Gadzooks — eventually. But every time I pictured him he looked so strange. He had his head bent low and his tail was all . . . droopy. The pages of his pad were peeling away. Where is he?" David peered around, hamsterlike. The pencil-chewing dragon was nowhere to be seen.

"Lucy took him upstairs," said Liz.

"Why?" David's tone was hesitant and nervous.

"Oh, you know what children are like. Maybe she was feeling sorry for him, him being a stupid dragon and all."

"He's crying, isn't he?" David said. He raised his head as if listening for the sniffles. "I made him cry, because the story didn't have a happy ending."

To his surprise, Liz shook her head. "Gadzooks would be a pretty poor authoring dragon if his flame was extinguished the first time he helped you with a sad story."

"*Extinguished?*" David looked at her hard.

"Dragons are different than you and me, David. When *they* shed tears, they fall within."

The tenant's face suddenly turned very pale. "You mean, Sophie was right: crying really does put out their fire . . . ?"

"Yes," Liz said. "Without flame, they enter a deep, dark sleep. If their fire isn't quickly rekindled . . ."

"No!" David sat up, grasping the blanket.

Liz, arms folded, sat quite still. "He's crying because you rejected him, David. If you love him, his spark stays lit, remember?"

The tenant's eyes filled with hope. "But I *do* love him — really. Where is he? I want to see him."

At that moment, Lucy slipped into the room. "Sophie's coming over tomorrow," she reported. "She says we've got to look after him. Puh."

"Tell me how to help Gadzooks," said David. "It has something to do with that story, doesn't it? The one about the last true dragon in the world? I heard you telling Lucy when Gawain was broken. He came to the stream to drink, and Guinevere sang him a sort of lullaby."

"The song of Guinevere," Liz said eerily, as Lucy began to faintly hum it, "is the key to the heart of dragon legend. Are you ready to dream it, David?"

"Yes," he said, pulling the blanket up to his chin. He slid down as Lucy's humming washed over him, closed his eyes and took himself back — to a distant time of fire-breathing creatures and cave-dwelling kin.

"Good," said Liz. "For you, and you alone, can rekindle Gadzooks. Listen closely, David. There may yet be time to save him. . . ."

THE FIRE TEAR

Like a flower blooming, she opened her hands. "The song of Guinevere touches the ancient heart of Gawain. It rouses his emotions, yet tempers his fire. Suddenly, he roars and shakes his head, then takes at once to the frosty skies. One beat of his mighty wings gathers leaves and dust into spiraling clouds. His giant shadow covers the valley. He bellows so loudly the icecaps shatter. The terrified villagers cower in their caves. Guinevere must surely die, they think. But when they look again, the red-haired girl is still by the stream. The dragon has flown, but a token of his presence is lying at her feet. It glints in the sunlight, green and ridged."

"A scale," whispered David. He pictured it clearly. It was about the same size and thickness as a roof slate, curved and tapering at the bottom.

"Guinevere holds it to her breast," said Liz. "A gift from a dragon is something to treasure. She knows, by this sign, Gawain will return."

"He knows she feels sorry for him," David muttered. "He knows she wants to help him."

"Yes," said Liz, "but he is not sure how. Even so, he comes to her again. For seven days and seven nights she sings her lullaby to the dragon. Sometimes he lies beside the stream bed with her. Sometimes he flies her to the ice-capped mountains. Her singing soothes his heart. But with every passing moon his strength is fading. The fire in his belly is losing its spark. One night he can barely lift his wings. Too weary to fly, he roves the valley, clawing at the earth, belching smoke. Soon, dragons will be no more. Gawain roars at the starlit sky and sweeps his tail in a whirlwind of despair."

"And the people," gabbled Lucy. "The people are coming."

"With spears," said David, creating the scene. "They want to kill him. While he's weak." He kicked his legs as if having a nightmare and felt a calming touch on his ankle.

"Even a dragon's dying breath could turn their bones to ash," said Liz. "Gawain stands forth. He scorches a line of fire in the earth. The villagers draw back, mortally afraid. Some hurl spears. They bounce off the dragon like pieces of straw. Guinevere, angered by the villagers' prejudice, runs to Gawain and swears undying love for the dragon. The villagers taunt her foolishness. They say she will die a lonely old shrew, for he, Gawain, is the last of his kind and little more than a fading ember. Guinevere knows this is true. But her will is strong and her heart is pure. She vows to find a way to preserve the dragon's fire. But who can she speak to about such a thing? Who knows the ways of dragons and men?"

"Someone old," said David, his eyes moving rapidly under their lids as if he was searching the valley for a figure. "Someone who remembers . . . lots of dragons."

"Gwilanna," whispered Lucy. "She goes to Gwilanna."

A picture shimmered into David's mind. Gwilanna: a smelly, broken-toothed crone; gray hair matted and blackened by ash; sitting in the mouth of a firelit cave, littered with bones and animal furs. "She's an outcast," he muttered. "People fear her. She's got scrawny hands and spooky eyes — sort of murky, like soup."

"Deeper than the ocean itself," said Liz. "She draws Guinevere into her cave. She already knows why the girl has come. 'You wish to save the dragon's fire,' she cackles. It is not a question, but a revelation of Gwilanna's powers."

"I don't trust her," mumbled David.

"Perhaps not," said Liz. "But the crone is Guinevere's only hope. Gwilanna spits a chewed bone into the fire. She demands that Guinevere give up the scale in exchange for the secrets she knows she requires. Guinevere opens her pouch. She has carried the scale since the day it fell from the dragon's body.

Gwilanna snatches it hungrily from her. She licks the scale with a snaking tongue, then beckons the beautiful Guinevere close. She caresses her hair with hawkish fingers."

"She's going to cut it," gasped David, "with the scale."

"One lock," said Liz. "In a flash, it is done. She rubs the hair once against the scale then hurls it into the crackling fire. Sparks fly to the roof of the cave. Somewhere in the distant ice-capped mountains, Gawain throws back his head and roars."

Hrrr, came a furious clamor from above.

David gripped the folds of the blanket. "It's loud. It's shaking the walls of the cave. I see dust and stones spilling out of the cracks."

"Dream it," said Liz, caressing the words. "Even a fading ember of a dragon can move the earth with the power of his breath."

"Hrr," breathed Lucy, as if to prove it.

"Now, the old woman takes Guinevere's arm. Her

fingers, like talons, cut into the flesh. 'You are joined to the dragon in fire,' she hisses. 'Now you must join him in water, too.' She points to the tranquil moon. 'His flame will expire when the moon is full. He will wish to die alone, as dragons should. But you must be there, waiting, child. For the moment will come when his fire will flow briefly into the world. The dragon is proud and knows no fear, but in truth he is crying deep inside. With his last breath, a fire tear will come. Catch it and the essence of Gawain will be yours; fail and dragonkind is lost forever.' "

"Fire tear . . ." David repeated tiredly.

"Dream it," Liz whispered, as Lucy began to sing once more.

David yawned and snuggled into his pillow, faintly aware of movement on the bed. It felt lighter, suddenly. More freedom to move. He stretched his legs and cuddled Winston. His body relaxed. His mind drifted. He saw Gawain on a mountaintop, silhouetted against the shimmering moon; Guinevere, wrapped in a kind of shawl, singing into the shell of his ear. Gradually, the dragon lowered his head. His spiked tail drooped. His scales fell flat. His oval eyes, long-closed and weary, blinked one final, fiery time. His life expired in a snort of vapor. But in that moment, a teardrop formed. A living teardrop, on his snout. A violet flame in a dot of water. It trickled down his face to the tip of his nostrils and fell, sparkling, into Guinevere's hands.

"Got it," muttered David, with a sleepy smile. "Umm. What happens now?"

His eyes blinked open. Liz and Lucy were nowhere to be seen.

"Liz?" he called, pushing the blanket aside. "Liz, where are you?"

He got out of bed and stepped into the hall. The house was wrapped in the silence of night.

David walked to the foot of the stairs, bathed in moonlight from the picture window. "Liz?" he called. "You didn't finish the story. What do I do about Gadzooks?"

Suddenly, something fluttered in the shadows and the moonlight was pricked by a faint orange glow. David gulped and glanced to his left. On the newel post beside him, two clawed feet were scrambling for a hold. A small, winged creature had landed there.

It was Gruffen.

KILNING GADZOOKS

Fff," Gruffen snorted and pointed his snout, hound-like, up the stairs.

"The den?" guessed David.

Gruffen blew a couple of smoke rings and nodded. He spread his wings and fluttered onto the tenant's shoulder. "*Hrrr,*" he went, warming David's earlobe.

"Thanks," David winced, and climbed the stairs.

As he neared the top, he turned his gaze toward the picture window. A frowning dragon was tapping the bulb of a small thermometer. It *hrred* warm air as the tenant went past. Meanwhile, in the bathroom, the dragon on the tank was blowing a beautiful rose-scented flame.

"I knew it," muttered David. "I knew you were real."

Gruffen flicked his tail as if to say "naturally," then *hrred* on the handle of the Dragons' Den.

The door to Liz's studio swung open.

David edged inside.

The reception was *warm*, but not exactly friendly. Claws tightened on every shelf as dragons stretched their necks to peer at the tenant. Some scowled with disapproval. Others whipped their tails. Before David could utter a word of explanation, one of the dragons gave a quiet sniffle. Gadzooks. He was sitting on the potter's wheel. Every pair of violet eyes turned to look at the story-writing dragon.

A strange hush fell. The room darkened as the dragons held their breath. David knelt in front of Gadzooks. The dragon had sagged into a doleful heap. His pencil and pad were lying idly at his side. Smudge marks had darkened the bridge of his snout as if he'd rubbed his eyes with his writing paw.

"I'm sorry I sent you away," David whispered. "Please come back. I love you. Really."

Gadzooks blew a pitiful wisp of steam. His head lolled forward and something glittered in the corner of his eye: a tear with a violet flame inside it.

There was a sharp intake of breath along the shelves.

Gruffen, still sitting on David's shoulder, let out a high-pitched squeak and whipped his book from beneath one wing. On the spine was a grand-sounding title: *Guard Dragons: Procedures for Beginners*. He flipped through at lightning speed, stopping at page ninety-seven. He blew what appeared to be toast crumbs off it, and rapped the page hard for David to see.

CRYING (not recommended for special dragons)

1. Take dragon to SAFETY

(Gruffen gave that a scorching check.)

2. In the event of a FIRE TEAR — catch it!

David, remembering the story of Gawain, cupped his hands and caught the tear as it dropped.

Dragons everywhere *hrred* with relief.

"What now?" asked David, for this was as far as Liz's story had gone. Guinevere had caught Gawain's fire tear — but what had she done with it? David rolled the tear in the center of his palm. The fire within it flickered and danced, throwing purple patterns all across the ceiling. On the potter's wheel, Gadzooks sank into a deep, dark sleep. Gruffen dug a claw into David's shoulder. David looked at the next instruction.

3. FREE the fire

He pressed the fire tear with his thumb. The tear spread flat but did not burst. He found a modeling stick and prodded it with that. The tear indented, but still it didn't burst.

"How?" he asked Gruffen. The guard dragon gave a worried shrug. From the shelves came a deep-seated *hrrr* of ignorance.

No one knew how to free the fire.

Then, with a clink, Gadzooks dropped a scale.

And suddenly, Gwilanna was in the room.

David and the dragons all reared back. A cloud of mist was swirling in the doorway, as if Gwilanna had dropped from the clouds.

"You must join the dragon in water," she cackled, snatching the scale as payment for her wisdom. She touched a grubby finger to David's cheek. A tear welled in the corner of his eye. Gwilanna screeched with laughter and disappeared. The tear trickled down David's face, then fell toward the fire tear in his palm. It dropped slowly, floating like a bubble. Inside was an image of Conker. The young squirrel tilted his head. He looked back at David as if he knew they would always be part of each other's lives. His eyes, no longer matted or cut, gave one single appreciative blink. Then the tears came together with a gentle *fssst!* and all that remained was a tiny flame.

There was no pain and the flame did not feel hot. It tingled in a light, refreshing way, touching every nerve in David's skin. He felt it from his head to the tips of his toes: dragon fire, burning within. Instinctively, he knew he could keep it if he wished. One inward breath would absorb the fire. But if he took it, Gadzooks would surely die.

You alone can rekindle his spark, Liz had said.

The fire belonged to the dragon.

David put the flame under the limp, green snout, watching it circle the cone-shaped nostrils. For a moment, little happened. The fire dipped and leaned and gave off a delicate flicker. Fearing it might go out, David decided to take a chance. Leaning forward, he blew on it gently, sending it spiraling into the snout. Gadzooks immediately sneezed, but somehow *inward* rather than out. His tail spike twitched. His scales rattled. He shuddered and coughed a wisp of smoke. His graying eyes turned through green to violet . . .

All around the shelves dragons flapped for joy.

Gadzooks's spark was lit.

Gruffen did a twirl on David's shoulder and hastily checked his book of procedures:

4. REKINDLE dragon

5. REKILNING strongly advised

Gruffen pointed to instruction five.

"No oven," said David, frowning a little.

Gruffen snorted and slammed the book shut. He pointed an excited paw at Guinevere.

Guinevere's oval eyes slid open.

Two rays of violet light poured forth.

She stretched her neck and looked down at Gadzooks.

Around the room, dragons began to trill.

Guinevere opened her stout front paws . . . and breathed a column of fire.

Hrrrrrr.

It engulfed Gadzooks in a ring of white light. The dragon twitched and lifted a foot. There was a crackling noise as his pointy ears rattled. A puff of steam came out of his nose.

Then Gawain walked out of the shadows. There

were gasps and much bowing of heads on the shelves. Gawain arched his mighty wings, leaned forward and blew a cone of flame. Gadzooks put back his head and *basked* in it. Within seconds, his scales began to lift. His tail curled up. His ridges straightened. The first luminescent flush came back to his glaze. Gawain roared and blew once more. In the window, the little stained-glass ornament twirled on its string and clinked against the glass. Orange light flickered around the room.

Gadzooks shook his head and sat up abruptly. He paddled his feet and thumped his tail. His scales clattered like a stack of dominoes. He stretched his neck in a graceful arc and fired off a happy-sounding *hrrr*.

"All better?" asked David.

Gadzooks gave a grateful nod. Gruffen fluttered off David's shoulder and handed Gadzooks his trusty pencil.

"What's that?" said David, pointing to the pad. There was some sort of tailed-off message on it. The last thing Gadzooks had tried to write.

"Wuz?" David muttered, reading it off.

Gadzooks shook his head. He licked his pencil and added three letters: z, l, e.

"Wuzzle," said David.

Gadzooks gave a radiant smile.

Outside, the first rays of morning broke across a sleepy Wayward Crescent. Inside, deep within David's mind, the light of inspiration dawned.

"Wuzzle," he repeated with a nodding grin. "Of course. *That's* how to end the story. . . ."

Maintaining
the Link

Sophie laughed so much her sides began to hurt.

"Cut it out," said David, sounding cross. "I'm telling you the truth, that's how she does it: The dragons kiln themselves."

Sophie pulled a tissue out of her sleeve and dabbed it twice against each eye. "David, you're making my mascara run."

"I'm not joking. Those dragons are *real*. They come alive when their eyes are violet." He glanced at Gadzooks, looking radiant in the window. "Show her. Go on. Flick your tail."

"Oh, stop it," Sophie pouted, shaking her fists. "You're just doing it on purpose now."

"I give up," David sighed, sinking onto the bed. He grabbed his guitar and twanged the strings, tunelessly.

Sophie leaned back in the computer chair and prodded him with an outstretched toe. "Come on, you had a dream, that's all. Granted, a very lucid dream, brought on by Liz's story perhaps, but it couldn't be anything more than that. Real dragons don't exist."

"They *do*," David insisted softly, hearing Lucy out in the hall. "Liz is just clever at hiding it. That lullaby they sing makes you think you're dreaming. I was there, Soph. I saw them. Honest."

Sophie crossed her arms and puckered her lips into a smile. "OK," she said in a high-pitched breath. "Next time we're having tea, I'll ask her. Hmm, lovely cuppa, Liz. Oh, by the way, we had a power outage yesterday — how do I get Grace to light a candle for me?"

"That's easy," David said in earnest. "Liz could do bonfires, never mind candles; she and Lucy have dragon fire inside them."

Sophie clapped a hand across her face. "And how did you figure *that* out?"

A shout from the kitchen stopped David's reply. *"Lucy, hurry up. It's clouding over. We're not having this ceremony in the rain."*

"Ceremony?" Sophie looked toward the window.

David stuffed his feet into a pair of sneakers. "Lucy wants to plant a tree for Conker — that horse chestnut she found in the gardens."

Lucy pounded past the door then, shouting, *"Should I get David and Sophie, now, Mom?"*

"Coat, first. It's chilly out there."

Lucy pounded back the other way.

"A tree. Ah, that's sweet," said Sophie. "It's nice that she's maintaining the link."

"They're the link," said David, pulling on a sweater. "I know what happened when the real Gawain died. When Guinevere caught his fire tear, she freed his fire — like I did with Zookie — but *she* didn't give it back. There was no point in trying to rekindle Gawain; they both knew it was his natural time to die. So Guinevere did the next best thing — she preserved their love by keeping his fire. And . . . dot, dot, dot."

Sophie glanced towards the door. "You're not trying to tell me that Liz *is* Guinevere, like she's a zillion years old or something?"

"No-oo. 'Course not. I think Liz and Lucy are —"

A child's fist banged on the door three times: *"We're going out to the garden now."*

"We'll be there in a minute," Sophie called.

"— I think they're Guinevere's *descendants*. I suspect Guinevere had a kid somehow and called it Gwendolen. That's why Lucy's dragon looks like her. Bet you any money I'm right. Both of them have got Gawain's fire. I wonder what it's like, being human with a dragon's spark inside you?"

"Like severe indigestion, probably," said Sophie. She stood up, gathering her hair into a scrunchie. "You know, you are really good at this. You should do it for a living. You'd make a ton of money."

"I'm going to," David said. "I'm going to write a story called *The Dragons of Wayward Crescent* next.

That Gwilanna woman's going to be in it. There's something very fishy about her. I want to know what she does with those dragon scales."

Just then the door clicked open and a hand launched Bonnington into the room.

"Go on, go get them."

Bonnington yattered something catty and sprang onto the blanket, yowling and fussing. Sophie picked him up and nuzzled his head. "Don't go prowling in the Dragons' Den, Bonny, Gruffen might scorch your ears and whiskers."

"He's in on it," said David. "*He* doesn't care."

Sophie laughed and put Bonnington down. "Don't listen to him, Bonny. He's nuts. Now, how cold is it? Should I wear my coat?"

David looked her up and down. "You look good as you are."

Sophie licked her thumb and rubbed a few cat hairs off her top. "David, we're planting a tree, not going out to dinner. Besides," she said, blushing, "it's nothing special." She was wearing a plain black T-shirt with a silver motif and matching black pants.

"Simple things suit you," David said, plucking a sheet of paper from his printer.

Sophie's eyebrows came together to form a slight scowl. "Don't spoil it. You were doing really well until then."

David moved a strand of hair from her eyes. "All part of my boyish charm." He grinned and placed a light kiss on her cheek. "You wait till Grace starts doing things, then you'll believe there are dragons in the Crescent. Come on, let's go plant this tree." He rolled the piece of paper and pointed to the door.

"What's with the paper?" she asked.

David looked across the room and winked at Gadzooks. "Just something we were working on before you arrived."

A TREE FOR CONKER

I hope this tree grows big and strong and makes us happy all day long — I learned that from Sophie," Lucy said. She hunkered by the hole she had dug beside the rock garden and dropped her conker into it.

"Very poetic," said Liz. "Can I water it now?" She tilted a watering can. A little spray of water jetted out of the rose, overshot the hole and sprinkled David's feet.

Lucy stood up, looking irritated. "Mom, we haven't filled in the hole yet." She crouched down again and piled in the soil, *then* invited her mother to water it.

Liz tilted the can again.

When the puddle had fully soaked in, Lucy announced stage two of the "ceremony": "Now, everyone has to say something nice."

"Such as?" said Liz.

Lucy planted her hands on her hips. "Such as, 'I hope this tree grows big and strong and makes us happy all day long.'"

"Lucy, I can't write poems."

"I'll say something," Sophie volunteered. "It's about Conker. Is that all right?"

"Yes," said Lucy.

Sophie locked her fingers together and cleared her throat as if preparing to sing. "Thank you, Conker, for bringing me into this wonderful house. If it hadn't been for you, I wouldn't have gotten to know Elizabeth or Lucy . . . or, um, who was the other person? Oh, yes — David!" She plopped a teasing kiss on his cheek.

"Your turn," said Lucy, looking at her mom.

Liz lowered her watering can to the ground. "I promise to take care of this tree and to always think of Conker whenever I see it."

"Good. It's David's turn now."

Everyone looked at the tenant.

David brought his hands into view and unrolled the

paper he'd taken from his printer. "I'd like to say something for *all* the squirrels. This is the end of *Snigger and the Nutbeast*. Second draft — specially rewritten." He lifted an eyebrow at Lucy. She looked at her mom, who pressed a finger to her lips.

"One blustery afternoon in the library gardens, Snigger was sitting at the edge of the duck pond, when Ringtail came bounding up.

'Have you heard the news?' Ringtail puffed. 'Cherrylea's going to have Conker's dreylings!'

Snigger sat up in surprise. 'I thought Birchwood was chasing Cherrylea.'

Ringtail kicked a flea from behind his ear. 'He was, until Conker came. Then he got all soppy and let Conker chase her around instead. Except that Conker couldn't chase her with his funny eye — so she let him catch up to her.'

Snigger cleared a knot of mud from his claws and spat it grumpily onto the ground. 'Pff! She never lets me catch *her.'*

'I don't blame her,' muttered Ringtail (but Snigger didn't hear)."

Lucy giggled into her hands.

" 'Where is Conker?' Ringtail asked.

'Wuzzled off,' said Snigger, as casually as he might crunch open a nut.

Ringtail's eyes almost popped out of his head.

'We were digging in the flowers near his tree,' said Snigger, 'when he jumped onto the grass, looked up at the library with his not-so-good eye, yawned a bit, said he loved it here and that he'd never been happier since he met me —'

'He must have chewed a bad nut,' muttered Ringtail.

'— then he stretched out and wuzzled right off.' "

"Oh, dear — I'm going to cry," sniffed Liz, fiddling in her pocket for a tissue.

Lucy slipped her hand into David's. "What happened next?"

David flicked his eyes back over the page. "Snigger

turned around. *The sun was beginning to set in the treetops, covering the gardens in a marmalade glow. 'The nutbeast and the little girl took him,' he said. 'They buried him, like a nut.'* "

A tear ran down Sophie's cheek.

"*Ringtail twitched his whiskers in approval. 'When I wuzzle off, I'm going to find a nutbeast,' he said.*

'*You couldn't find an acorn in a plant pot,' joked Snigger, and he whisked away with Ringtail in pursuit.*

Away they bobbed, under the willow trees, into the clearing toward the great oak. High above, the sun winked in the pale October sky. Leaves tumbled freely in the wind, filling up the paths and flower beds and lawns like pieces of a slowly forming jigsaw puzzle. Beneath the tall horse chestnut tree, a cool breeze rustled over the ground. Somewhere in the distance the library clock bonged. A mallard quacked. A pigeon cooed. The sun sank gently over Scrubbley. And the library gardens, like Conker, were at peace. The End."

"Hooray," cried Sophie, applauding loudly.

"Beautiful," said Liz, blowing into her tissue.

Lucy, still holding David's hand, swung it gratefully back and forth. "I like that ending. It's much better than the other one you wrote — but I still think Birchwood should have helped Conker build a drey in the hollow in the tree near the notice-board."

"I can edit it," David sighed.

Lucy smiled and leaned against him.

He bumped her gently with his hip. "We did our best for Conker, didn't we?"

"Yes," she said. "We'll do our best for *any* animal in this garden, won't we?"

"I think so."

"Promise?"

"Yes, I promise."

"*Really* promise?"

"Cross my heart and hope to marry a frog."

There was a pause, then Lucy said, "I saw that hedge-hog yesterday."

David's face went pale. "Oh no," he said.

But long before the words were out of his mouth, he was glancing back at his bedroom window.

Spikey

Gadzooks jotted down on his pad. And what's more, he underlined it.

Twice.

THE END

THE END

ABOUT THE AUTHOR

Children sometimes ask me, "How long does it take to write a book?" The answer usually varies from one hour, for little books, to several months, for novels. This story, *The Fire Within*, has taken nearly fifteen years. This does not mean that my dragon wrote it longhand on his trusty pad and I merely copied it off him. It simply took a long time to "filter through" as authors tend to say. David Rain is me — when I was young and daft and I really could boast a mop of brown hair. Nowadays, I have more gray hairs than a squirrel. I like squirrels. I met some once in the Churchill Library Gardens in Bromley, Kent. They ate my sandwiches. That's squirrels for you. As for dragons, hmm. If you really want to know about dragons you will have to invite me to come to your sch— Oh, just a minute, Gadzooks has a message . . .

Gruffen says hrrr

Tch. Gruffen. Flitting about again. Just wait till Gretel arrives, he'll have to behave himself then. Who is Gretel? Ah, that's another story. I suppose I really ought to scribble it down. In the meantime, please enjoy this book. If you love scribbling as much as I do, I hope you find your own Gadzooks one day.

Love and best wishes,

hrrr